P9-BJC-692

TEXAS TEASE

Yankee carpetbagger, murderous rebels, and hot-tempered women—that was what McCoy found when he rode into Johnson Creek, Texas. But Spur had stepped into vipers' nests before, and he knew there was only one thing to do—gun them down before they got a bead on him.

SPUR #20

TEXAS TEASE

DIRK FLETCHER

LEISURE BOOKS NEW YORK CITY

A LEISURE BOOK®

February 2005

Published by

Dorchester Publishing Co., Inc.
200 Madison Avenue
New York, NY 10016

ISBN 0-8439-2475-6

The name "Leisure Books" and the stylized "L" with design are trademarks of Dorchester Publishing Co., Inc.

Printed in the United States of America.

Visit us on the web at www.dorchesterpub.com.

SPUR #20

TEXAS TEASE

1

A rifle snarled to Spur McCoy's left and in the same instant a bullet sang by his head sending the U.S. Secret Service agent diving off his mount and twisting to hit the ground on his hands and feet. He had been moving through a small patch of black oak and mesquite along a little dry stream bed. He hadn't noticed any other rider nearby.

His right fist raked the six-gun from his holster. Another shot came, higher this time, far over his head into the branches of an ancient cottonwood above.

Spur's horse ran on for a dozen yards and stopped, head down grazing on the new spring grass that still showed green through the weeds and leafmold.

Spur looked around. He was in at the edge of the fringe of trees that had sucked enough nourishment to flourish along this little stream that ran full in the fall when the rains came. He had not seen nor heard anyone since he rode in out of the hot sun a few minutes before.

He crawled forward toward a foot-thick black walnut tree and looked around it from ground level in the direction of the rifle report. Through the light brush and a few oak branches he saw a partially hidden rider on a white horse. The mount moved toward Spur cautiously.

Spur's six-gun came up when he saw a rifle aimed in his general direction. Brush and cottonwood leaves covered most of the rider and horse. He pondered shooting through the light cover. No, the smallest twig or branch could deflect a pistol bullet. He had to wait and be sure.

His trigger finger tightened to half-pull as he tracked the rider past a small oak and into the open beyond the low brush.

When McCoy saw the rider plainly, he swore. The rifleman was a woman. She hadn't noticed him or his horse although she could easily see the mount grazing twenty yards away. Instead she concentrated on the branches of a tree just in front of him. She lifted the rifle and shot again. Spur saw that it was a small bore weapon.

"Oh, damn I missed!" she wailed, then looked around as if to see if anyone had heard her swear and giggled. Quickly she ejected the round and pushed another one in the single shot weapon. At least it was new enough to use solid cartridges.

Spur stood up behind the tree and stepped into the open. She sat her horse astride like a man, not twenty feet away. She wore a soft green blouse, a small cap over brown hair and a brown skirt.

"I won't shoot if you don't," Spur called.

She started from surprise, triggered the weapon and sent the bullet slamming into the ground a dozen feet in front of Spur. Then she looked at him and her surprise turned into a smile.

A big jackrabbit leaped from high grass near where the rifle bullet struck. Its long ears laid back as it took three running hops and vanished behind some brush.

"Oh, dear, Daddy would scold me for sure. I'm terribly sorry, I really didn't mean to fire at all. You frightened me, and I jumped and nearly fell off Prince here and then my finger just . . ." She paused and watched him closer. "Good, I think you're smiling."

"That's the second time you've shot at me. The first time you missed by a good six inches."

"Oh, dear. Did I really?" She swung down from the horse with a practiced move. She wore a divided skirt to facilitate her riding.

She walked the white mount toward him.

"I didn't intend to shoot near you, I thought I was alone out here. I often come hunting squirrels—not to hit them, just to see how close I can come. And you? You're a stranger around Johnson Creek."

She waved her hand toward the start of the little town that could be seen across the flat Texas panhandle perhaps half a mile to the north.

"Yes, a stranger and I'm just coming to town. If you promise not to shoot at me anymore, I'll risk catching my mount and riding on."

"I promise. I'm going back to town, too, may I ride along with you?"

McCoy nodded and they walked toward his horse where it kept munching on the tender young grass. He watched her for a moment. She was a mite of a thing, barely five feet tall, with rich brown hair that fell out of the cap and down over her shoulders. He guessed her eyes were brown too. She was slender, even in the riding skirt, and showed small breasts under the blouse.

Her sweet smile snared his attention. She had a delightful, innocent, remarkably pretty face. Her eyes sparkled as she watched him. He guessed she must be nineteen or twenty.

"Really, I won't shoot at you again. I won't even load the rifle. My daddy gave it to me on my tenth birthday and taught me to use it. I'm a whole lot better at target practice then I am at hunting. I don't like to kill animals.

"You haven't told me your name. I'm Beth Johnson, and my grandfather started the town. Yes, *those Johnsons.* Do you have a name?"

McCoy laughed. He told her his name and that he was going to the little town on business.

She put one hand on her chin, sizing him up. "Let's see, about six feet and two inches tall and two hundred pounds. Reddish brown hair, a thick, full moustache and mutton chop sideburns. A rugged, outdoor face with dangerous green eyes. Your hands aren't tough enough for you to be a cowboy, no rope burns. You're too nice to be an outlaw, and I know all of the U.S. Marshals up here in the panhandle. No sample cases so you can't be a drummer."

Beth lifted her left foot into high stirrup and swung into the saddle on the white mare. She scowled at him for a minute as he caught the reins of his mare and settled into the leather.

"I give up. You're Spur McCoy, but I don't know what line of work you are in." She grinned. "I'm just naturally curious, that's all." She whipped the white mount around and galloped for a hundred yards toward town, then turned and waited for him as Spur walked his bay up to her.

"You don't like racing. Maybe you're a gambler?" She shook her head. "Nope, your vest isn't fancy enough. I give up."

They rode along in silence for a while. She kept glancing at him. At last a slow smile began to grow. "Oh, yes, I have it! You're the new man who is coming to run the hardware store. You look like a reliable merchant type.''

"Sorry, Beth. I wouldn't know a twenty penny nail from a come-along.''

"Oh.''

"But I do have business in town. I've heard of a Harry Johnson. Are you any relation to him?''

"Yes, he was my father. He died, was murdered, two weeks ago.''

"Murdered? Harry Johnson?''

"Yes somebody shot him five times, while he lay in his bed. I heard the shots, and by the time I got there . . .'' Beth looked away and rubbed at her eyes.

"I'm sorry, Beth. He was the one I was coming to see, but don't tell anyone I said so. You ride on ahead. I'll come see you later today.''

She wiped her eyes, nodded. "Only if you'll help me find out who killed him. I must know. The town marshal here is worse than useless.'' Her face was composed now, and took on a serious stern strength that caught him by surprise.

"Of course, that's part of my job now, to find out who killed your father.''

"Come see me at the bank.''

"Which one?'' he asked.

"The only one, the Johnson Bank. It's mine now. I'm the banker for most of the county.'' She kicked the white horse with her heels and it lunged forward and raced the last hundred yards into town.

Spur McCoy came in a quarter of a mile around by a different road. The first thing he wanted was a cold beer.

Johnson Creek, Texas was about as he had guessed from the size and location. One main street where all of the town's businesses were located. The commercial section was almost two blocks long with a good-sized Catholic church at the far end. There were clapboard houses, mostly one-story tall,

11

spreading back on right angled streets from Main. A few more than four hundred souls called this place home.

He found the town's one hotel, Johnson House, a three-story affair painted a soft brown, with a stoop and a porch big enough for three all-weather captains' chairs on each side. He tied up at the hitching rail out front, stepped up six inches to the boardwalk and went up the steps with his small carpetbag in his left hand.

Spur McCoy had learned to walk like a mountain cat, always alert, ready to move any direction at any time, observing everything that went on around him. Immediately aware of any danger. He felt none now. Nobody knew he was coming to town. Still the man he had come to see had been viciously murdered with five rounds.

It was not a good way to start a case.

He signed in under his own name at the desk, and asked for a second floor room with a window on Main Street. That way he could keep track of what happened. As he signed his name, the clerk craned his neck to read it. He was jittery, so nervous his hand almost shook. After he read Spur's name he calmed down enough to take money for the room.

Spur paid three dollars and fifty cents for the room, for seven nights. At fifty cents a night he knew this was not Houston. The room was barely worth fifty cents. The bed springs sagged under the lumpy mattress, the mirror over the small wash stand was cracked, and so was the china washbowl.

The room may have been ten feet square, but he doubted it. A small dresser and one chair completed the furniture. But the window did open on Main Street. He stood there a moment looking out. He saw the young woman, Beth Johnson, whom he had met outside of town, leave one building, cross the street and go into another store.

The second business was the bank, a solid looking structure of brick, two stories, set on a corner.

Yes, the rich young girl with the rifle. He dug into his carpetbag and shook out a clean shirt, stripped off his dirty one and his kerchief and gave himself a half bath in the cold water of the wash basin.

Then he shaved, combed his hair, put on the clean shirt and his second vest of brown doeskin, and perched the low crowned brown hat on his head. The hat had a string of Mexican silver coins around the crown. One of them had a bullet hole in it.

Across the street in the Lucky Horseshoe saloon, he tilted a cold bottle of beer and grinned at the apron.

"Settles the trail dust," Spur said.

The barkeep was big, heavy and surely worked as the bouncer when needed. He nodded at Spur's comment. "Figured you was new in town."

He felt it again, an undercurrent, a tension. It was as though half the folks in the town were holding their breath waiting for something ugly to happen. He'd noticed it in the room clerk. As he had walked across the street one woman gave him a wide berth and two men stared at him hard, almost in confrontation. He had passed the incidents off as his being a stranger in town. Now he wondered.

A man got a beer from the barkeep and slid a dozen feet down the bar away from Spur.

"Friend, this doesn't seem to be a particularly neighborly kind of town," Spur said.

"Some say."

"People seem like they got some bad tasting grub in their craw and they can't spit it out."

"Been known to happen. You want another beer?"

Spur shook his head and the apron moved away. McCoy spotted a poker game at the side of the saloon. Poker players were a good test of a community.

He walked back to the game, saw a vacant chair and stood behind it. "Mind if I sit in for a few hands?" McCoy asked. "New money into the game."

For a moment no one replied. Three men at the table looked at the fourth, a rangy man with sunburned face and rope scarred hands. He shook his head. "Sorry, this is our last game."

Spur nodded as he eased away from the table and went back to the bar. He ordered another of the stubby beers. When the apron set up the drink, Spur's gaze held him.

"What's happening in this town? Every person but one I've met so far is wound up spring tight about to explode."

"Town's got some troubles, but me, I try to stay out of them. Lost one eye at The Wilderness, don't aim to fight anybody else's fight from here on. Got me enough trouble with the dam deadbeats cadging drinks."

"Fair enough. The Wilderness, that wasn't trouble, that was disaster for both sides. Where can I find the sheriff?"

"No sheriff here, he's at the county seat. We got a town marshal, such as he is. Down Main Street a block and a half. Next to the stage office. Can't miss it."

Spur finished the short beer and went out the door with a wandering step. Nobody in this Texas high plains country seemed to be moving any faster than required.

He watched the people as he moved along the boardwalk. Most were quiet, reserved, smiled if they noticed his big grin. But no one stopped to chat, ask about the news from wherever he came from. They were only worried faces staring back at him.

He passed two general stores, a small freight office, then a meat market with a half a beef hanging in the window. Next to it was the Centennial Barbershop and a saddle maker. A saddle in the small display window looked like an excellent example of a real craftsman at work.

He passed a well stocked drug store, and then came to the stage office and the small sign over the next doorway that said simply, "Johnson Creek Jail." He went in and found a counter across most of the ten foot wide room. Behind it stood a man six inches shorter than Spur. He wore a black hat, vest and jacket and a Colt .44 hung in a belt holster that was hitched up so high it would be awkward to draw.

"Looking for the marshal," Spur said.

"You found him. I'm Marshal Ludlow."

"I just rode into town on business, and I can't figure out what is going on out there. The whole town seems ready to blow apart. There's a tension in the air that's almost like lightning."

"Local problem, none of your concern."

"What's the problem?"

"None of your affair."

"Marshal, it is my affair. I'm about ready to get my head blown off by some hothead with a hogsleg and you say it doesn't concern me?"

Marshal Ludlow paced slowly around his small office in back of the counter. Spur saw a door that led to some jail cells in back. When Ludlow stopped moving he lifted his hands palms up.

"The war's only been over for four years. Feelings are still running high in the South. Now we get this Bagger in town and he brings with him fifty voting citizens, everyone of them black. He gets himself voted in as town mayor. He's a Carpetbagger of the worst kind. Lots of southern towns and cities are having trouble with Carpetbaggers from the north. We'll deal with him eventually, in our own fashion."

"That explains part of it. Baggers, I've heard plenty about them." He also had a sheaf of papers detailing how he, as a federal law officer and enforcement agent, had to bend over backwards to be sure that the Carpetbagger northerners and their black associates were given total protection under the new laws.

Ludlow watched him.

Spur shrugged. "Fine, at least I know. I don't want to get in no trouble here. Came on business, do my business and move on, or stay."

"What kind of business you have to do here?"

"Retail. Hear there's a hardware store for sale here."

The lawman snorted. "You don't look like a store man. Not with that tan and sunwhipped face. Besides, you wear your six-gun too low on your thigh. Only one reason, for a quick draw. I've seen a few like you. Don't like fast guns around here. Best if you do your business fast and get out of town."

"An order, Marshal?"

The smaller man watched Spur for a moment, then his glance fell and he turned away, looking smaller. "Mostly I make suggestions. Mostly they get followed. Up to you." But his voice had lost its snap. His lack of self confidence showed plainly. But a coward's backshooting a man makes him just as dead Spur knew.

"Thanks, Marshal. I'm not at all opposed to taking suggestions. Now, one more thing. Where can I find a gent named Harry Johnson? I'm a long-time friend of Harry's. He invited me up this way to see his town and his daughter and his bank."

"You don't know?"

"Know what, Marshal?"

"Harry Johnson died about two weeks ago. Tragic really. He'll be missed around this town."

Spur watched Ludlow critically, but there was no hint that he knew more than he was saying.

"From what Doctor Greenly said, he had some stomach problems and then something ruptured. Died in just a few minutes in the middle of the night."

"I'll have to visit the family. Is there a widow?"

"No, just his daughter Beth. She's probably at the bank this time of day."

Spur thanked him, strode out of the office, and marched down the street toward the bank. He was headed there but he saw the office of the local newspaper across the street. That would be his next stop. Why had the local doctor covered up the murder? Was it really murder or had Beth Johnson been making up little girl stories? There was one quick way to find out.

2

Spur angled across the dirt street to the *Johnson Creek Record.* The newspaper office was narrow, squeezed in between the barbershop and the Habberman Meat Market. The sign on the outside looked new, but it wasn't, just well painted.

Inside he found the usual counter across the room that was only fifteen feet to the wall. A double door led into the backshop and pressroom. Nobody was in the front office but he heard activity.

"Back here," a voice shouted from the rear.

Spur went around the counter and through the open door. The newspaper plant smelled as they all do, slightly musty, and overpowering with the unmistakable odor of newsprint, paper stock and printer's ink.

The back shop was slightly less stocked than many he had seen, but it was adequate, with a one-sheet flat bed press that was hand cranked.

Standing next to the type case was a man in his late forties, blond, with a plain, open face behind wire rimmed spectacles, a big nose and slightly protruding teeth.

"Breaking down last week's front page. What can I do for you, stranger?"

As he spoke the man pulled solid rule slugs from the wooden form that held the type and headlines for last week's front page of the *Record*. Then he picked up a handful of the small metal pieces that each had one letter formed on the top. Automatically he read the letter and dropped it in a designated bin in a type case in front of him.

"You must have a good memory where each letter goes," Spur said.

The man's expression never changed. "Nope. Just habit and practice. Rote really. Been casing type for twenty years. They tell me I did the whole front page one night while I was sleeping."

Spur grinned. "Two jobs at once. My name is McCoy, and I'm wondering if I could take a look at last week's paper to catch up on what's happening in town."

"That's why I print it. I'm Hans Runner. Cost you a nickel for the paper."

Spur found a dime in his pocket and laid it on the edge of the front page form.

"Keep the change. I'll get a paper out front. Mind if I read it here?"

"Help yourself." The man hesitated. "We don't get many strangers around here. Is there a story for the paper why you're in town? Maybe interested in the closed up hardware store? We sure could use that place being open."

"Might be, looking around a bit. Is it a good store? Why is it closed?"

"Right good little hardware. It's got things nobody else carries in town. We ain't a big town and a hardware store is one we need. Closed? Oh, old

19

Charley took sick last winter, lingered on for a while, finally got pneumonia and died overnight. No kin that we know of.''

"I'll look it over." Spur went back to the front of the office, found the stack of this week's paper and scanned the front page. There was no death story about Harry Johnson. He looked around, found a rack that held previous editions. They were neatly punched with three holes and held between half inch thick sticks that bound them together.

He took off the current one and checked the front page for the previous edition. It had been two weeks since the paper came out. The story was the lead with a banner across the top of the page.

"Harry Johnson Dies at 52. Son of Town's founder succumbed last night to a sudden stomach malady that took him quickly according to Dr. Greenly. The physician said he was summoned about midnight, and by the time he got there, Mr. Johnson was bleeding internally and there was no possible way to save his life.''

Spur read the rest of the story. Nothing was said about any violence, or shots being fired. The town marshal was not mentioned. A simple, unexplained, sudden death of a man in his prime.

Another item on that front page caught his eye:

"Mayor White Defends Position." The story under the headline said: "Major Don White today denied that he is an opportunist from the North, who came to Texas to take advantage of the reconstruction laws. He said he is here for the long term, that he loves this town and is fighting to make it better in every way.

"He pointed out that he has already established a free public library, that he is considering gas lights for some of the Main Street areas, and that he will strictly control gambling, and all saloons and that the town will not tolerate fancy women.

"Critics say that White is little more than a Carpetbagger, here to fill his own pockets at the city's expense. They point out that he had himself voted a $200 monthly salary, when the previous mayor served for nothing. White said a professional manager for the city is needed and must be paid for.

"Dr. Greenly, one of Mr. White's continuing critics, says that everyone knows that Mr. White won the election because he brought in fifty Negro men and registered them to vote under the new federal reconstruction laws. Before the fifty men arrived in town from the Houston area, Dr. Greenly says there were only eighty-three men registered to vote in the city.

"Twenty local men, mostly drifters, who had never voted before and could not read nor write, were scooped up by Mr. White and registered, then paid to vote the way he told them, Dr. Greenly charged. This gave Mr. White an unbeatable total of seventy sure votes.

"Since many men were out of town on election day or ill or failed to vote, the total vote in five previous elections had been an average of 56. Last election a total of 114 voted. The mayor won election over his opponent 82 to 32.

"Dr. Greenly said he is investigating the state law on election fraud, and may call for a new election if he can prove that the votes were obtained under ' incentive or duress.' "

Spur read the rest of the story quickly. "Baggers," he said softly. Carpetbaggers from the North. Hundreds of them swept down on the South to use the new reconstruction voting rights of the newly franchised Negro voters and virtually take over whole cities and counties. Carpetbaggers had produced more hard feelings than anything since the war ended.

He turned back to the current paper and saw a story on the front page. "Man Shot Dead, Riot Ensues." The story told how a black man had been shot while trying to steal a bottle of whiskey from a local saloon. The head shot killed him and he was laid out on a door outside the saloon with a warning: *Baggers who steal get kilt dead. Go home Baggers or Else!*"

The mayor and a dozen of his black friends protested to the town marshal. Marshal Ludlow looked over the situation and said it was his opinion that the man had been shot while committing a felony, the barman was not charged since the body was on private property, he could not remove it without the consent of the property owner.

A short time later the story said, thirty enraged and armed black men stormed into Main Street, recovered the body of the dead man and took him to the cemetery for a funeral.

Spur read the rest of the paper closely. There were two more incidents of robbery that were laid to the new blacks in town, but there had been no charges brought. The mayor had intervened in each case and repaid the loss.

Now Spur understood the tenor of the town. There was a real crisis building here. The townspeople had suffered about all they would under the Carpetbagger. Even now the fuse might be lit and burning somewhere. Spur went back to talk to the newsman.

"These Baggers been around for a while?"

"Too damned long, but we haven't figured out a way to get rid of them yet without a lot of bloodshed. Right now things are heating up.

Wouldn't wonder that the top might blow off in a week or so. Just sort of feels that way."

"You lived here long?" Spur asked.

"I know this town. Been here for ten years or more now. Thought the town would grow more than it has. I'm just scratching to hang on. Now city taxes went up again."

"Mayor White's doing?"

"Damn right. He got four new city councilmen elected. All blacks, and all do exactly what he tells them. Three of the four can't read nor write. But they can talk."

"White controls the vote?"

"Every time. He said we needed something called Public Welfare. Says a person who is blind or deaf and can't support himself, should get help from the town. Says if a man can't find work to feed his family, the town taxes should help him.

"Now he's got 45 of those 50 blacks on this Public Welfare. Us taxpayers handing out a dole to them blacks every day so they can sit on their asses and make jokes about us. Ain't the American way!

"Don't mind feeding Mrs. Giersbach, cause she's blind and got no kin, but to dole out good money and food to folks to sit around and play poker all day for matches, just ain't right. Folks around here about had a bellyful.

"You can feel the tension out there on the street. Blacks don't even come down town much anymore. And the good blacks we had here before, now don't know what to do."

"This whole thing must be bad for business," Spur ventured.

"Damn right! My ad space fell off twenty percent in the last six months since White's been here. And I didn't have that much more to start with. Taxes are just too high. One store closed down, mostly because of taxes."

Runner put down a handful of rule slugs in a tray at one side of the type case and wiped his forehead leaving a smudge of black ink. He pulled out a new font drawer of larger sized type and went to work casing the headline letters and numbers.

"Ain't right, what he's doing. Sure we lost the war, and we paid for it. Hell we pay every day. I just don't think Abe Lincoln wanted us to pay this way. His getting shot probably was the worst thing that ever happened for the South, next to losing the war, of course."

Spur folded the paper and put it under his arm. "Doesn't sound like a favorable climate to open a new business in, does it, Mr. Runner?"

"No sir, Mr. McCoy, much as I hate to say it, sure don't seem like it. I could sure'n hell use your advertising and printing work, too." He pied a column of type and began casing the individual letters. "Hell, maybe it'll work itself out. I'm staying right here, I damn well know that!"

Spur thanked him and walked back on the street, glad to know a little more about this powder keg of a town. He just hoped that he would be around in the right place to stamp out the fuse if it started burning.

He went up the street to the brick bank building and stepped inside. It had two teller windows protected with iron cages and a long counter separating the bankers from the customers.

A door to one side led into an office he guessed would be that of the president . . . Beth Johnson.

He walked to one of the cages and asked to see Miss Johnson. The teller took his name and asked him to wait. A moment later Beth flew out of her office smiling at him. She wore a conservative loose fitting blue dress that covered her from chin to wrist to toes.

"Mr. McCoy! I was hoping you would stop by. We have a lot of things to talk about. Please, come into my office."

Inside the large room she closed the door and softly threw a bolt locking them in. When she turned her smiled had bloomed even larger.

"Why didn't you tell me about the Carpetbaggers?" he asked sharply.

She lifted her head defensively, brown eyes taking on a hurt look. Then she shot up her brows and shook her head. "I didn't think it mattered that much. Besides, with too much trouble here, you might have wanted to leave town. I need you to stay. The whole town of Johnson Creek needs you to stay."

"First I have to know who is lying here. You tell me your father was shot five times. The marshal, the doctor and the newspaper say he died of a stomach problem. Are you lying, or are they?"

"They are. Doctor Greenly got here just a few minutes after the shooting, and he said there was nothing could be done for Daddy. Then he carefully explained to me that since Daddy was trying to get the Carpetbaggers and the townspeople together on this big conflict, that we needed to be careful.

"If we said Daddy was murdered, each side would accuse the other of doing it. And the whole thing could flare up into a war. I don't want anyone else to be hurt. Daddy tried to work out the problems between the sides. He just couldn't."

Spur walked around the office, looked at some of her father's pictures and mementos on the wall she hadn't yet got around to removing. He looked at a heavily curtained window. Then he came back to where Beth stood behind the big desk.

"All right I believe you. There is a cover-up, but we don't know why. The reasons the doctor gave are ridiculous. Why did he really want it hushed up?"

"It could have been a hot head from either side who did it. I don't see why there were five shots, but maybe he just wanted to make sure."

Tears seeped from her eyes. She walked slowly to him and put her arms around his back and pressed tightly against his chest. Her head barely came to his chin.

"Spur McCoy, I need you desperately here. The whole town needs you. I . . . I'm willing to do anything you want me to do, if you'll only stay and help me find out who killed my father."

She stepped back and began unbuttoning the fasteners of her dress.

"Beth, you don't . . ."

She stopped him by reaching up and kissing his lips. For a moment her tongue washed his lips through her open mouth, then she came away. Quickly she opened the buttons and pulled the dress apart. She lifted the chemise showing her small, round breasts with light pink areolas and small pink buds of nipples.

"Spur McCoy, I'll make love to you right now, right here, anyway you want me to. Don't you understand? I desperately need you to find my father's killer!"

She caught his head and pulled it down so his mouth touched her right breast. Spur kissed the orb, moved to the other one and kissed it, then lifted up and kissed her lips softly.

He pulled her chemise down to cover her, then adjusted her dress and buttoned it.

"I'm staying. Don't think you can bribe me with your delicious, sexy body. It looks like I have a lot of work to do here, and I need to get started. I want you to help me, but not by laying on your back. I need your memory, your knowledge of the town and its people."

"Yes, yes, I'll help." She turned away and stamped her foot on the floor. "Damn!" She looked up and smiled. "Damn, it wouldn't have been that big a sacrifice for me. Did it ever occur to you that I might have *wanted* to make love to you, just for the pure, wild, sexy pleasure of it?"

Beth turned at once and went behind her desk.

"Mr. McCoy, would you sit down right here and we'll start to work on our problem. Ask me anything you want to know about this town, I've lived here all my life. I know everything there is to know about Johnson Creek."

Spur stood watching her. He went around the desk, lifted her up and kissed her hard and demanding, his hand covering one of her breasts and massaging it gently. He let the kiss last a long time, then he broke it off and went back to the front of the desk.

"That's a small sample, something we can look forward to sometime in the future. Right now, we do have a lot of work to do."

For a moment Beth was in a soft, wonderful world that she didn't want to leave. Then she blinked and saw Spur across her desk. She remembered his kiss, his caress of her breast. Yes, it would be something to look forward to.

She smiled, blinked again. Then she leaned toward him. "Mr. McCoy, I will look with delight every day to the future. Now, I believe you said we had some work to do. What is it you need to know about Johnson Creek and its people?

3

Beth Johnson looked at Spur McCoy for a moment and smiled softly. He had said later. Good.

"Now, about our town. Seven months ago Don White came into Johnson Creek with his fifty Negroes. He registered them to vote, registered himself and legally put up four of his people for city council seats and himself for mayor.

"For a month he went around town registering every drifter and no-account he could find who would vote the way he was told to for five dollars. He found plenty.

"When the election came he won by a paid for landslide. Every one of his people voted. We've been trying to do something about it ever since with no luck. He's made changes, increased taxes twice and as you know has all his blacks either on the city payroll or on a dole from the city.

"Dr. Greenly said if White works the way other Carpetbaggers around here do it, he'll try for some big contract or cash award and abscond with all the city money he can grab, leaving his coloreds in the lurch."

"Does it look like he'll do that?" Spur asked.

"I'd think so. Everything points that way. But he's slick. Butter won't melt in his mouth."

"His four city councilmen, do they count?"

"Only to vote. Only one of them can read or write. They do what he tells them, nothing more."

"Any hope on the city council?"

"Only Zed Hiatt is left from the old town council. Five votes on the council. Zed isn't a brilliant man. He's a widower and a jeweler. Quite good at designing jewelry, but no push, no starch in his backbone. He never fights the majority, simply votes no and they charge forward."

Spur scowled, paced the room and watched her.

"The town marshal. I take it he's hired or fired by the city. So he must be working closely with Don White."

"Not really. He was marshal before White came to town. White let him stay on, nobody is sure why. Public opinion, maybe. White tells Ludlow what to do and usually he does it. If he didn't that would be cause for firing him.

"Garth keeps to himself a lot. He was away for a while in the war and then came back, wounded. Lost an eye, I think. He does the job. It isn't that hard in Johnson Creek."

"Deputies?"

"Usually he has one man on nights. The night man sleeps in the jail, so can handle most of the problems. Not much doing here after about ten o'clock. That's when the saloons have to close. New law by the new mayor."

"Who else should I know?"

"June. You have to meet June. I bet not even you could walk away from June Black. June is a seamstress here in town. Twenty-one, maybe

29

twenty-five, nobody knows. She's a breed, but not the usual kind. June had a black mother and a Kiowa Indian father.

"A pretty girl, sultry, and . . . Well, you'll see. She knows everything about both sides in town. She's also the nearest thing to a fancy lady we have. She accepts some special male visitors now and then, but on an exclusive basis. Expensive, too, I've heard."

"Would she know much about White?"

"Not from that angle, he's got a little black chitty of his own. She looks like she's about thirteen, but she could be fourteen. Her body is at least twenty-five!"

"June is a social outcast then, but still makes dresses for the uppity women in town who can afford it?"

"Right. And she's a good seamstress. Let's see, who else. You said you've met Hans Runner. He's a character. Has a wife, but nobody sees much of her. He runs the best paper we've had here in years."

She paused and looked out the window. She had opened the drapes so the sun would shine in.

"You should know about our whiskey priest. The Catholic bosses somewhere sent us a priest who couldn't be tolerated anywhere else. He uses more Communion wine than any other churchman in history, but prefers his drink to be much stronger.

"The story is that Father Desmond was chased out of his last parish after one of the women in the church told the bishop that the priest had accosted her, had his way with her when she went to his quarters for special guidance."

Beth walked around the room, her hips working smoothly under the blue dress. Spur did not miss her subtle way of showing off her best features.

"That's about the best gossip on the people I think might be able to help you. They all know more than most about what goes on in town. Do you want me to go along with you, introduce you to them?"

"Why don't you introduce me to the priest, after that I'll be on my own."

She smiled. "Sounds safe enough. Right about now he should be in his quarters or in the chapel. Let's go."

They went out the front door, and she held his arm as they negotiated the dirt of the street, angling around a fresh pile of horse droppings. Dirt and manure in the street were common factors in every Western town, and Spur had grown accustomed to them.

They stepped up a foot to the boardwalk on the far side in front of a closed store, when a woman came screaming out the front door.

She shrilled at the top of her voice. Her dress was half ripped off, one large breast sagged from her bodice and blood showed on her face. Spur grabbed the woman, Beth pulled her dress around to cover her and Beth nodded toward the bakery next door.

They hurried the woman inside and the baker motioned them into the back room where there was a chair. Beth took over, helping the woman sit down, blotting perspiration from her forehead, all the time talking calmly to her.

She had stopped screaming as soon as Beth put her arm around her and helped her into the bakery. Now tears came, huge gasping sobs that shook her.

Beth asked her gently what happened.

"They raped me! Two of them black baggers. They caught me in the alley, dragged me inside and . . . and did it. Twice, both of them twice!" She began crying again. The baker had been listening.

He took a six-gun from a drawer in the bakery and hurried out the door.

Too late, Spur realized what he was up to and he nodded to Beth and went after the baker. He was far too late. The baker must have shouted the news as soon as he hit the street.

Everywhere men grabbed at weapons, women and children darted off the street into the first store they could find.

More than two dozen men, all armed with pistols, rifles and shotguns prowled Main Street.

Spur ran for the jail. The marshal met him on the way out.

"I know, I know. Something like this is hard to stop." He ran up the street and fired his six-gun five times into the air.

"There will be no violence here!" he shouted. "The guilty men will be found and punished. Now go back to work, back to your homes, all of you."

Three men ran around the corner from Second Street. They had in tow two blacks. Ropes were around the colored men's necks and they were naked to the waist.

"Got them, by Jesus!" one of the white men yelled. "Drunk as skunks, both of them. Found them hiding in the old store where they done it. One didn't even have his pants back on yet."

Marshal Ludlow looked at the three men, solid citizens all of them. He stared at the two blacks.

"You do that white woman? You raped her in the old store?"

Both stared at him and wouldn't reply.

"Lynch the black bastards!" one man roared.

Spur's six-gun blasted into the air. "Enough of that kind of talk. We've got laws here."

"Wanta see Mista White," one of the Negroes said.

"You can talk to him in jail," the marshal said. Neither of you has denied that you raped that woman. You're both under arrest."

Someone in the crowd cheered. Another man yelled for a hanging.

Spur watched the crowd of more than forty men now. He motioned for Ludlow to take the prisoners away. Spur walked behind them, facing the crowd. His Remmington .44 drawn and covering them.

"The first man who gets any ideas about gun play is a dead hombre," Spur said. The crowd slowed.

Ludlow pushed the two black men through the jail door, slammed and locked it. Spur watched as he closed the two-inch thick inside shutters on the window. Then he looked at the crowd.

"It's a matter for the law now. Break it up here. Get back to your jobs or wherever you were. The excitement is all over. Move out, now!"

They scattered but slowly, watching the jail.

Somebody at the far end of the crowd yelled for a hanging, but Spur couldn't tell who it was.

Before they had walked fifty yards up the street, they heard a volley of shots coming from a half block farther on. Spur and the rest of them ran up to the corner of third, but found nothing.

Too late, Spur realized his mistake. A diversion! As he turned there came four spaced shots from behind them, near the jail. They raced back that way and found the two Negroes on the boardwalk in front of the jail. Both had been shot twice in the head from close range and were dead.

Inside the jail, Marshal Ludlow lay on the floor, still unconscious from a blow to the back of the head. The rear door into the jail and the door to the alley were both open. Someone had surprised the marshal.

By the time Spur brought the marshal back to consciousness, Don White stormed into the jail.

"Stop them! For God's sake, stop them! The ghouls are parading up and down Main Street with the bodies of those two boys. Get out there and stop them Marshal Ludlow, or turn in your badge!"

Garth Ludlow blinked as he looked up at White. Then he rose slowly to his feet, weaved as he tried to get his balance. Then he tore the badge off his shirt and slapped it into the mayor's face.

"Take your goddamned job, and your badge. I quit." He walked out the front door and Spur followed him. Spur looked toward the yelling and shouting up the street. The parade turned and the wagon hauling the bodies came down Main Street toward Spur.

Two men led the horses and the cheering. Spur put one shot into the air, then twenty feet away shouted into the sudden stillness.

"Hold it, right there, if you want to move another step, you're doing it over my body." Slowly he holstered his gun and stared at both men.

"You both have iron, let's see if you can use it. Right now, both of you draw and fire, or get the hell out of the street."

The two men were from a ranch. The only thing they had ever shot at were jackrabbits and rattlesnakes. They backed down and hurried into the crowd.

"Get the undertaker!" Spur bellowed. "The rest of you have thirty seconds to get off the street or I'm hauling you in to jail. Vamoose!"

Before the undertaker got there, a black man

hurried in from the side street. Mayor White talked with him a moment, and then both got on the wagon and drove down the side street and out toward the cemetery.

The curious, the angry, the ordinary citizens came out of the stores and talked in low tones. They had no idea who this gunman was who took over and stopped the violence, but some cheered him silently. Maybe he was the one who could save the town from the Carpetbaggers.

The mayor came back and called to Spur.

"Mr. McCoy, I'm told you've called. I want to thank you for stopping this thing. It could have become ugly."

"I'd say two rapes and two murders was already ugly, Mayor. What are you going to do about it?"

"What can I do?"

"You could give this town you stole back to the citizens and go return to wherever you came from. You're an opportunist of the worst kind, White. I'm surprised that you don't slit your own throat one of these mornings when you're shaving. How can you live with yourself? How can you stand to look into the black soul of that man in the mirror every morning?"

Spur spun on his heel and strode away. He heard more shooting and charged up the street into the scene. A black man had just been shot coming out of a store. Before anyone could move, a white couple coming down the street in a carriage was shot dead by a rifle.

Spur grabbed a rifle from a man standing on the sidewalk and blasted four shots into the air.

"Now listen to this!" he bellowed. Every head turned and the three blocks of Main Street were suddenly quiet.

"My name is Spur McCoy. I'm a United States Secret Service Agent from Washington D.C. I'm taking over the law enforcement of this town as of now. There will be no more gunplay in Johnson Creek starting now. Anyone carrying a weapon will be arrested. No guns are permitted in public view. The next person who fires a weapon will be arrested."

He stalked to the boardwalk and caught the man who he heard bragging that he had killed the Negro. He slammed the rifle out of his hands, twisted one arm behind his back and marched him to the middle of the street.

"This man is under arrest for murder. Anyone else who fires a weapon in town will also be arrested. Now get about your peaceful business."

Spur turned his back on the majority of the people and marched his prisoner to the jail. There he found the deputy who heard about the marshal resigning. Spur ordered him to stay on duty and to find a second deputy for the night shift.

Spur stood outside the small jail a moment. Things were not going well. How could he find out who killed Harry Thompson in the middle of a damn riot? He shrugged. Maybe the whiskey priest could help him calm the people. That was his next stop.

4

Spur McCoy scowled as he saw the luxury of the Catholic church in this dirt poor town. The faithful suffered in this life so the church could have a real gold dome and an altar that was worth as much as half the town. The grounds were watered and well tended, undoubtedly by many volunteers.

He pasted a smile on his face and approached one of the dark robed sisters who showed him where Father Desmond was. He was in his quarters at the back of the complex. The only priest in the parish had a six or seven room apartment attached to the small parochial school.

Spur knocked on the door and waited. A few moments later the heavy panel opened and a short man on the heavy side stood there in clerical collar and shirt, but no black jacket.

Father Desmond was fifty-two, had a tick that bothered his left eye, and a flat Gaelic face, and soft blue, watery eyes. His face was sallow white, with a liver spot on his right cheek. He had not shaved that morning and dark stubble patterned his jaw.

"Yes, you're the new man in town. Maybe you can

37

do something about this bunch of Godless Carpet-baggers we have." He held out his hand. "I'm Father Desmond. I understand you want to talk to me."

"Fact is, I do, Pastor. If you have the time?"

"Now is a good time, come in, my son."

Spur was on the verge of flaring up, declaring that he was not Catholic and he was not the man's son; instead he stepped inside the pleasantly cool and well furnished room.

Father Desmond closed the door and motioned for Spur to sit on one of the sofas in the big room.

"Now, I hear you've been talking with our marshal, the newspaperman and pretty little Beth Johnson. This must be about the Carpetbaggers, right?"

"Partly. I understand you know just about everything that goes on in Johnson Creek. That's why I wanted to come and see you."

The priest laughed lightly and in the gush of air, Spur smelled the tinge of whiskey breath.

"You flatter me, Mr. Spur. Through the confessional, I do have an ear to much of the communtiy, but that is shared only with God. However, there is much else in town that I am aware of, and that I hear about."

"Pastor Desmond, I'm a peace officer, a U.S. Secret Service Agent working for the Federal Government. There are some problems in this town that local authorities can't solve. We were called in to help. I'd appreciate all of the cooperation I can get from you."

"Anything I can do, Mr. McCoy, to help the people of Johnson Creek, I feel it is my duty to do. What are you concerned about besides the way the Carpetbaggers are looting our town?"

"First the baggers. Do you have any influence with the town council?"

"No, absolutely none. Not a one of them is Catholic. Zed Hiatt was a shirtsleeve Catholic, but fell by the wayside years ago. The black men are Baptists, I think, and Don White is an atheist. I can't be of much help there."

"All right, Pastor. The other problem is Harry Johnson. He wrote me a letter. Said he had something that he wanted to confess. Now I'm not sure how Johnson died. The marshal and the doctor say he died of stomach problems. But a witness says there were shots heard. Just how reliable are the doctor and the marshal? Could they be covering up something?"

Father Desmond had reached for a wine bottle on a small table near the sofa. He paused and frowned. When he picked up the glasses they jiggled together. Slowly he poured wine into the two glasses and handed one to Spur.

"A good, robust port wine is good for digestion. Now, about how reliable those two men are. I've never had any cause to doubt the word of either one. I know them only casually, but they seem like reasonable, steady men."

Spur sipped the wine. He was no expert, but this was not a bargain bottle off a shelf. He watched the priest. The blue, watery eyes held steady.

"All right, Pastor Desmond. You know why I'm here. If you hear of anything that I should know that will help on either case, you'll be doing the whole town a favor by telling me."

Spur sipped the wine again, set down the glass and stood.

"Now, I better be moving. I have a lot of people to talk to today."

The priest stood as well and led the way to the door.

"If I discover anything that seems important, I'll be sure to contact you."

Spur eased his hat on at the door, touched the brim and walked out into the sunshine.

Behind him, the priest closed the door slowly, then he locked it. He moved with a sudden tiredness as he headed for his big bedroom at the end of the hall. There he stepped inside and his face broke into a smile.

Calida stood by the bed. She had just finished making it up. She wore only a short petticoat of cotton covering her slender young form, her rich black hair fell to her waist. She looked at Father Desmond and love and devotion bled from her eyes.

Calida's face was round, small, her eyes jet black, her nose sculptured and pert in a pretty face. Now her smile was dazzling.

"Should I stay?" she asked. Her English was good. She had been orphaned and raised by the sisters since she was two. She had grown straight and true and developed breasts the nuns had been surprised by. Now they thrust against the thin petticoat, her nipples already hard and pulsating.

"Yes, I need you now more than ever."

She sat on the bed waiting. He tugged at his clerical collar. She sprang up to help him.

He began talking then, talking to her, to a congregation, to his bishop, to the Pope. Even talking to God.

"Calida, I am a sinner, you know that. You know my vices, my weaknesses. Probably the whole town does. I know they call me a whiskey priest. Still I can say Mass. The bishop sent me here to get me out of his way, so I wouldn't embarrass him or the church.''

As he talked she slipped off his shirt, then worked at his belt and the buttons on his fly.

"God knows I have tried!" he shouted the words. Her hands fell away from him for a moment. "I have tried to serve God! There were just so many other desires. Oh, sweet God . . . desires! I have had so many. I have been sorely tempted so often, and fell just as often.

"I can't refuse a lovely woman, one of the first ones? Ah, when I was younger and much stronger. It was my first parish, and she was the wife of a man who traveled a great deal. She came to confession and pleaded with me to absolve her of wicked thoughts, of a fantasy that she had been making love to a neighbor.

"After the confession, I walked in the church garden. It was a large church and I was only one of several priests. I realized that she always came to confession when I was in the box. She found me in the garden and took me behind some hanging vines and we made a secret place and she kissed me. Then I kissed her and she told me I must make love to her or she would explode. She opened her bodice and put my hands on her warm breasts, and then I couldn't stop.''

Calida had taken the rest of his clothes off. She sat beside him still in the petticoat waiting. Gently he reached for her, kissed her sweet lips, then lifted the petticoat over her head.

He gasped in pleasure at her beauty. Her body was that of a young goddess: perfect legs, a tiny waist, surging upward thrust breasts so young and proud and heavily tipped with soft pink nipples that quivered as he stroked them.

"Ever since that first time, Calida, I have been a sinner in the eyes of God and man. In San Antonio I even defiled a young nun. She became pregnant and left the order quietly. We both knew she was not destined to be a nun.

"But was I to be a priest? I wrestled with that problem for years. Oh, I said Mass, I gave the sacraments, but was I worthy to be a priest?"

"I was here during the war as you were growing up."

He fondled her breasts, then lay down on the bed and she lay close beside him. He kissed her breasts.

"Near the end of the war something happened which I had trouble even then explaining, and now it is a misty, uncertain nightmare for me."

She kissed him, pushed him on his back and rolled on top of him as she had done so often before. Her breasts hung delightfully over his face.

"Then, Calida, two weeks ago, the whole ugly, terrible nightmare rose up again, and again some stranger took control of my body and made my hand do a terrible thing, and I will never be the same again!"

Calida lowered a breast to his mouth.

"Father, don't talk that way. You frighten me when you talk like that. For a while you used to do that, then you stopped. No more."

He was quiet for a moment, then he kissed her breast and sucked it into his mouth.

"Yes! Father! I will make you feel good again. Please let me make you feel better!"

Without waiting she found his erection and lifted and shifted her young hips as she had done so often before and lowered onto him. Then she moved slowly at first, then faster and faster, riding him like a pony, bringing him quickly to a climax.

When his panting and quivering and thrusting were over, he pushed her away and sat on the edge of the bed.

Father Desmond began to cry. Soundlessly at first, then with racking sobs and gasps as he let the pain and the anger and the shame flow out of him.

She held him as he quieted, his tear streaked face looked at her, and he began sobbing again.

"I had no right to defile you, too!" he whined through his tears. "No right. I am evil. I don't deserve to live."

A knock sounded on his door.

"Yes?" he said.

"Father, Mrs. Ortega. She needs you. Her husband says it is time for the last rites."

"Yes, Sister. I will be there shortly."

"She is dying, Father, you must go," Calida said softly.

"Soon, soon." He looked at his Calida again, so young, so pure, so beautiful! He touched her breasts and felt them burning with her desire. He bent and kissed them and then he forgot everything as he made love to Calida again on his bed, even as Mrs. Ortega came closer and closer to death.

He stared at the wall. He had sinned again, the sins of a priest! He was sure now that he did not deserve to live.

He lifted away from Calida, kissed her sweaty forehead and told her to rest. Quickly he dressed and slipped out the door. Sister M. Wanda led him down the corridor.

"Mrs. Ortega is still failing. She is waiting for you to come before she dies."

Father Desmond nodded and hurried through the back gate of the church grounds and over two streets to the small Ortega house. It had only a wooden box for a table and two chairs in the first room, and a makeshift bed in the second.

Mrs. Ortega saw him and she smiled. Quickly he gave her the last rites and she smiled again, reached for his hand and kissed it. Then she looked at her husband, smiled again, and died.

Her husband shook his hand and thanked him. Father Desmond left the house quickly. How could anyone have such faith? Long ago he had argued with himself that the entire idea of religion was a myth, the creation of the mind of man. That all religions around the world were based on fear . . . fear of death. He had laboriously traced them back to their foundings, and each one carried the same theme, magic and myth, fear of death and the search for a reason for life.

Little by little he had come to the conclusion that there was no reason for life. All the trappings and grandeur, all of the organization and platitudes and rituals and traditions of the Catholic church were simply another means for deceiving the poor and the ignorant.

Where did that leave him? He was either a cynical manipulator of the innocent, a monster deceiver and a charlatan or he was so ignorant and stupid that he couldn't recognize the truth about religion when it slapped him in the face.

Father Desmond walked slowly back to the church.

He was not stupid or ignorant. His teachers had told him that. They doubted sometimes his dedication, his "call." Lies, all lies! The Catholic church was truly a huge monolith perpetuating itself. A monster of a religious business reaching all the way to Rome!

How had he lived with himself being such a pious hypocrite all these years?

Calida had made it possible lately. Before there had been others willing to lay with him. Some thought they defiled him, others were sure they were piling up credits in heaven that would show up at the pearly gates in St. Peter's log book. What a surprise for them when they died and never woke up! When they knew for sure that dead is dead. That there is nothing else to life but life itself. When it was over . . . it's over!

He laughed. How simple, how stupid people were! How like little children!

How terrible his transgressions against humanity! He had not transgressed against God, since gods were figments of man's imagination. Like the Romans. We scoff at the idea of a thousand Roman gods.

We laugh at the animism gods of the primitives in many lands. But five thousand years from now, will not the intelligent men of that day, howl with glee at the ridiculous mythology of Christianity that millions of people believed in, and many died for?

Father Desmond walked slowly to the rear gate of the church yard. So many volunteers kept the gardens beautiful. A labor of love. He too had a labor of love.

He went into his quarters, told Calida that he was feeling tired and could not say the five P.M. Mass. He wanted to be alone this evening. He kissed her cheek and told her to go and read a good book.

Father Desmond walked slowly into his large bedroom, locked both doors, took out a bottle of whiskey and a pitcher of water and proceeded to drink himself insensible as he lay on his big bed, alternately laughing at the stupidity of man, and crying for the lost love of God.

5

When Spur McCoy left the Catholic church and Father Desmond, he headed for the building he had seen marked as the city offices. It had to contain the mayor's office. It was time Spur had it out with the duly elected mayor.

Spur McCoy walked confidently. He was as Beth had estimated a little over six feet two and about two hundred pounds. He was a crack shot with pistol or rifle, an expert hand to hand fighter with fists, knife or staff.

His outdoor work kept him constantly on the go and tip top physical condition.

After Congress established the Secret Service in 1865 to protect the currency, Spur had applied and become one of its first agents. Before that, he had served the last two years of the war in Washington D.C. as an aide to long time senator Arthur B. Walton of New York.

Spur walked another block down Main and saw the city offices.

He had not always been in the West. Spur was born in New York City where his father was a

wealthy merchant and importer. Spur went to
Harvard and graduated when he was twenty-four
years old. After that he worked for his father for two
years in some of his businesses, then took a commission in the Army during the war.

He served six months in the Secret Service's
Washington D.C. office before he was assigned as
chief of the Western division of the service, with an
office in St. Louis. His responsibility was everything west of the Mississippi.

With such a big area, he was constantly on the
move. At first the Secret Service was the only
federal agency that could enforce Federal laws.
Which meant the service quickly expanded from its
role of hunting counterfeiters, to working on any
type of federal crime.

Spur walked into the city offices and asked to see
the mayor. A small, black-haired woman with her
hair in a severe bun on the back of her head asked
his name and announced him.

Don White looked up from his desk and a stack of
papers Spur guessed had just been put there for
effect.

"Ah, Agent McCoy. I never had a chance to thank
you for the excellent work you did this morning in
controlling what could have been a full scale riot.
The city thanks you."

"White, I didn't come here for any thanks. I want
to know how soon you can be out of town?"

A huge black man Spur had not seen sitting in the
corner of the room leaped to his feet, his hands
holding a double barreled shotgun that had been
sawed off.

"No," White said sharply. "Willy here gets
nervous when anyone uses that tone of voice with
me, Mr. McCoy. As you know, I am entirely and

47

perfectly legal here. I was voted into office by a majority of my constituents. The new Federal election laws specify that all Negroes be allowed the right of the vote without any exclusions.

"I for one, intend to see that those laws are carried out, and that my Negro brothers get to use their vote franchise."

"White, you know damn well you don't care a bit about all that. You're here for power and money. But most Carpetbaggers head for bigger towns. How is there much for anybody to steal here in Johnson Creek? That's what I can't figure out."

"Don't try, it'll strain your small brain. All you have to do, Federal lawman, is make sure that the newly enfranchised voters who are with me and those long time residents of this small town, maintain their right to vote. That's your job, lawman." White grinned at Spur.

"Now if you don't have some official business, I'm going to ask Willy here to help you leave."

"Willy might wind up with a broken face if he tries," Spur said evenly, so softly that Willy couldn't hear.

White snorted. "He'd make kindling out of you. Just walk out and don't break up any furniture."

"Where's the big money, White? That I can't figure. It's easy to see how you stir up the people, let your Negroes run wild in town without their women. That figures. But it's the money, your payoff for all this work, that I can't figure out where it's coming from."

Spur walked toward the door. "Where you from, White?"

"I'm from Johnson Creek."

"Before that, New York, Baltimore?"

White laughed. "Chicago."

"That figures, too. You were a nothing in the big city. So you heard about the Carpetbaggers and you decided to get in on it before it was worn out. You're almost too late, White."

Spur heard the snap as a shotgun meshed barrel and stock as it was ready to fire. He turned and looked at the armed guard.

Willy grinned at him.

"Double ought buck," Willy said. "From here with both barrels, I can damn near cut you in half."

"No, Willy," White said. "We'd have a dozen Federal agents down here within a week. We don't need that."

Willy lifted the shotgun, disappointed that he wasn't going to get to use it.

"Walk carefully, Mayor White," Spur said. Then he turned his back on both of them and marched out the door and to the street.

As Spur moved he filed away what he had seen. There were four black men sitting at desks in the city offices. White must have moved some of his men in those jobs. He wondered if they got done, or done right.

He cut across the street, sidestepped a prancing black pulling a fancy buggy, and went up the wooden steps to the Johnson House Hotel. When he asked for his key at the desk, there was a note under it. The clerk gave him both and turned away.

Spur read the note. It was from Beth:

"Spur McCoy. I insist on your coming to my house tonight for a small dinner party I'm giving. The address is 124 South First Street. Casual dress will be fine. I'll expect you promptly at 6:30 so cook will not be angry. If for any reason (except death of course) you can't attend, I shall be forever angry and furious and disappointed. See you at 6:30 . . . Beth Johnson.''

He looked again at the note, then drew his pocket watch from his trousers and checked the time. Already it was past three. He had missed his noon meal somewhere along the way. He wasn't worried. He could miss any two meals a day and function at top efficiency.

Spur went up to his room and sat by the window staring down at Main Street. Why had Harry Johnson sent that letter to Washington? What was it he wanted to confess that he could not trust to the local government? He wondered if the Carpetbaggers were the cause of that distrust, or was there some deeper, more serious problem?

Could the whole thing have anything to do with the just finished Civil War? The fighting had been over scarcely four years. Old angers, old hatreds were fading slowly from that titanic struggle, and would never die out until the participants themselves were buried. There was little actual war action in this section of Texas. A few border raiders perhaps.

The raiders were not a proud part of the war for either side. Most of them had regular Army leadership, but they gathered their forces from the rabble of those times. Many of the raiders on both sides were little better than outlaws and killers who pirated most of the booty for their own uses, and little of the supposed gain actually reached the participating armies.

Raiders, he would remember that possibility.

Spur lay on the bed fully clothed and pondered his problem. The priest had been no help. He probably knew nothing, and was more wrapped up in his own problems and hanging on to his play acting role as a religious leader.

The marshal, now the ex-marshal, had not indicated in any way that shots had been fired into Harry Johnson. There was a chance he didn't know it, if the doctor had taken the body directly to the undertaker.

It was after four when he went to the bank. It was closed. He went on to the Johnson place and rang the bell. A slightly flustered Beth Johnson answered the door.

"You're early," she said. Her brown hair was mussed, she wore a long robe and a frown.

"We need to talk. I want to know exactly what Dr. Greenly said to you the night your father died. We can do it now before the dinner."

She held the door open and waved him inside. "First you sit and read some of father's books, while I finish dressing. You are very naughty coming so early before a lady has a chance to get herself ready."

"You look fine."

"Oh, damn! I don't want to look just fine, I want to look gorgeous! Now stay in the library until I put myself together."

Spur found himself in the man's room, a combination library and den, with two walls filled with books. All had been filed alphabetically according to the author.

He found some classics, some Shakespeare, some poems by a man named Longfellow, and some from a new writer by the name of Mark Twain. On another shelf were books by Walt Whitman, and more poems from Emily Dickinson. Harry Johnson had a wide interest in his reading. Spur picked up a volume by Bret Harte, a collection of some of his short stories.

Spur settled down to the opening story, *The Outcasts of Poker Flat.*

"As Mr. John Oakhurst, gambler, stepped into the main street of Poker Flat on the morning of the 23rd of November, 1850, he was conscious of a change in its moral atmosphere since the preceding night. Two or three men, conversing earnestly together, ceased as he approached and exchanged significant glances . . ."

Fully a half hour later, Beth Johnson appeared in the den doorway. The gown she wore was expensive, finely tailored and cut low in front not so much revealing her bosom, but displaying the fact that there was little there to reveal. Her hair had been lifted up on her head and pinned in place with a few ringlets around her ears and on her forehead.

"What a marvelous transformation!" Spur said, dropping Bret Harte, eager to get on with his questions for Beth.

Beth blushed. She curtsied, then looked up at him. "It is just a dress I got a while back, and . . . I wanted to look . . . nice for you." She came in and sat down in an upholstered chair near the short sofa where he sat.

"You had some questions?"

"Tell me everything that happened the night your father died."

"Everything . . . well. It was a normal evening. We had dinner, then I played the piano for a while and father read. We both went to bed early and that's the last I remember until later that night when I woke. I have no idea what time it was.

"Voices. I heard three or four different voices.

52

They seemed to be arguing, and they came from down the second floor hallway where my father's room was. At first I thought I was dreaming and tried to go back to sleep. But I heard them again.

"I decided to get up. As I hunted for my robe I heard the shots. A number of them. I wasn't sure how many. Then there was nothing but silence.

"By the time I got my robe on and hurried down the hall, I found my father's room door open and his lamp burning. Inside Daddy lay across the bed on his back. I could see the blood on his face and his hands, and then on the sheets under him."

She stopped and covered her face. "It was horrible. I knew that Father was dead. All that blood. But I hurried downstairs and roused our cook and told her to get dressed and rush over and get Doctor Greenly. She was back in a short time, saying she had found the doctor on the boardwalk as she passed Main Street."

"It was maybe five minutes after she left the house that Dr. Greenly was here. He took over. Made me leave the room, examined Daddy, then came out and told me."

"How did he tell you, Beth?"

"First he said Daddy had died. There was nothing he could do to help him. I cried and cried, and when I stopped, Dr. Greenly said he had Daddy taken to the undertaker. It would be best that way.

"That's when I asked him who shot my father. He said what shots? So I told him earlier in the evening I had heard some men arguing, and then later some shots three or four, I wasn't sure."

Beth stood and paced up and down in front of the sofa, looking at Spur now and then.

"So, Dr. Greenly said he didn't want to tell me, but my father had been shot, murdered. He didn't want to worry me. And he said it would be better not to tell anyone right now. He said with all the anger in town over the Carpetbaggers, it would be best.

"Daddy was trying to get both sides together to try to work out the problems. Dr. Greenly said a hot head from either side could have killed Daddy. He said if we made an announcement about it, each side would blame the other and the whole thing could blow up, like I told you before.

"I fought the whole idea, but I was tired, and drained, and he convinced me not to say a word about it. Not just yet."

"Did the newsman, Hans Runner, say anything about your father being murdered rather than dying of natural causes?"

"No. I'm not sure that he knew. Dr. Greenly might have told him what he wanted him to know for the story in the *Record* the next week."

She looked out the window. "The day of the funeral a strange thing happened. The undertaker took me aside and said he knew the doctor said natural causes, but he found five bullets in my father's chest and stomach. He dug them out. Two were .44's or .45's and one a .32 and one a .38 and the last one an old minnie ball. He said it was none of his concern, but he wanted me to know."

Spur sat up straighter. "Five bullets, which could have come from at least four and probably five guns. Did five men shoot your father that night?"

"I just don't know what to think. I haven't said anything yet, but I was about ready to when I shot at you in the brush."

Now it was Spur's turn to get up and walk around the room. "Why would five people shoot one man?

It doesn't make sense. One shot or two will usually kill a person. Why five?"

"That's what I've been trying to figure out ever since."

There was a knock on the door.

"Dinner is ready, Mr. McCoy. May I take your arm?"

"Just don't go too far with it."

"What. Oh, a joke. Yes. I'll only take it to the dinner table."

They went down the hall to a dining room and at once he saw that the table had been set for only two.

"When you say a little dinner party, you do mean it is going to be small and exclusive, don't you?"

"I'm a selfish person. I don't believe in sharing. And tonight I want you all to myself."

"I think that is taken care of. Now, some more questions. Did you hear any words or sentences when the men were arguing? Even a single word might be important."

She frowned as he sat her at the luxuriously laid out table. He sat across from her. She shook her head.

"Nothing. I figured at the time it was a dream, so I didn't bother remembering any of it."

"All right. Now, did your father have any enemies, the kind who might kill him?"

"No! That's why this is so grotesque. Certainly not five men who wanted him dead so badly that they would all shoot him. There is simply no one!"

"Wrong, Beth. There are five out there in this town. Make me a list of what your father did for recreation. Did he play softball on Saturdays, go fishing, ride horses, build fancy buggies or practice shooting pistols in his back yard. I want a list of

everything he did, every organization he belonged
to, what committees and groups he worked with.
Let's do that right now."

Hilda, the cook came in the door with the first
course, a green salad with an interesting dressing.

"Let's wait on the list. First I want to stuff you
with fine food."

The meal was outstanding, and as they had ice
cream and cookies for dessert, Beth made out the
list of her father's groups and organizations. It was
short.

"The Board of Trustees at the Congregational
church, City Election Board, the County Planning
Commission, and the Home Guard, but that was
disbanded just after the war."

"Hobbies?"

"Pitched a mean game of horseshoe, liked to ride,
do those fancy show horse things. He was on the
Merchant's Association Board and a member of the
Road Commission. For a while he used to play poker
once a month, but I'm not sure they kept up the
game. That's about it."

"You're sure."

"There might have been a State Banker's Group,
I'm not certain there." She paused. "Let's go into
the living room. I love a fire in the fireplace. And it's
still cool enough out nights to make it feel good."

Spur hestitated and Beth groaned.

"Damn! Won't I ever learn? This is one man who
will not be rushed. So don't rush him. Just be nice
and look pretty and don't let him know that you'd
die for a good night kiss . . . even."

Spur laughed. "Hey, sometimes rushing can be
fun. But right now I've got a million things to check
out. I am supposed to be working you know. Any-

body else I should see on your list of locals who know the town?''

"Yes, Big Paul Smith, our saddlemaker. He knows everyone, is a friend to all, and is the best leather man in six counties. He usually works late. Stop by now and see if he's open. He's just down from the jewelry store the other side of the bank.''

At the door Spur touched her shoulders, then picked her up and kissed her gently on the mouth and put her down. For a moment she didn't move.

"Could we try that again when I'm ready for it?''

Spur grinned and bent down and kissed her again. This time her arms came around him and the kiss was one of fire and meaning.

When she let him go, she leaned against the wall and smiled.

"Oh, boy, now I'm sorry I didn't try to rush you. Don't stay away long.''

Spur grinned, kissed her forehead and went out the door and down the front walk to the street. He had a late date with a saddlemaker. The questions kept bothering him. Why would five men shoot the same man and why did the doctor try to cover it up? The doctor's logic for the cover up was laughable. But it wouldn't be if the doctor was one of the men who shot Harry Johnson.

6

The Secret Agent strode down the middle of the dusty, dark Johnson Creek street. There was little moon, just a slice. He looked up, checking for the Big Dipper and North Star. The Dipper was hanging sideways to the left of the North Star. The handle was almost overhead with the pointer stars angled in from about where the eleven number was on his watch.

That would make it somewhere around eight P.M. By four A.M. the dipper would be rotated almost to the bottom point where the six hand was on a watch. The dipper swung around the North Star once every twenty-four hours. Cowboys doing nightriding on a herd of cattle called the Big Dipper their star time Waterbury.

Spur checked the boardwalks. There were half a dozen men loafing or walking along past the closed stores. Most of them moved from one saloon and gambling hall to the next.

Spur saw the bank and headed toward it across the street. He passed the Silver Dollar saloon and as a shaft of yellow light shone on him from one of the big windows. When the light bathed him, a shot snarled into the Texas night air.

Spur dodged to the side and dove behind a big rain barrel at the near corner of the saloon. Two more shots flared from the edge of the alley. Both rounds struck the barrel and penetrated the side, but died in the water inside.

Spur came up firing his Remmington .44, blasting three shots at the mouth of the alley, then charging toward it along the protection of the front of the saloon.

He sent a drunk sprawling as they collided outside the swinging doors to the saloon. Spur kept his own feet and flattened against the corner of the saloon. He peered around into the darkness of the alley.

Someone ran the other way.

Spur jolted around the corner of the saloon and plunged into the inky depths of the darkness. He paused, his heart racing, his breath coming in quick gasps. Through it he heard more steps ahead, slower this time.

He thumbed the three spent rounds from his revolver and pushed in four new ones . . . he had six shots now. He fired twice at the footsteps, then surged to the other side of the alley as he charged forward.

Again he paused, listening. A baby cried somewhere. A woman shouted something at a man who laughed.

He moved forward on cougar paws, not disturbing a rock or clod, not even moving the air before him. Twenty feet down the dark alley, he heard something. Two deep buildings came all the way to the alley, but a short one allowed a thirty foot hole between them.

In that dark place someone moved again. Spur

held his Remmington as far to the right as he could reach and fired into the black place between the longer buildings. As soon as he blasted one shot he jumped to his left to put him well away from his own gun's flare.

Three shots in quick succession blasted from the black hole between the longer buildings. The lead was all ticketed for Spur's muzzle flash, where the bushwacker thought his victim still stood.

That was what Spur was waiting for. He returned the fire with his last three shots, bracketing the attacker's muzzle flash.

When the sound of the gunfire trailed off, Spur could hear a man's low scream of desperation. He waited. The man could be faking him into a trap.

Then Spur heard a death rattle, the last surge of air from dead lungs. Nobody could fake the deadly sound. Still he moved forward slowly. Then in the slice of moonlight he found the man pitched backwards, face up, one hand holding his chest where blood had seeped but was now stopped.

Somebody came out of the rear door of the business.

"What in tarnation is going on back here?" a man asked.

"Bring a light," Spur said. "I think a man just died."

The store owner brought the light and the undertaker. Spur had never seen the dead man before. He was white, about thirty and had the rope scarred hands of a cowboy.

The merchant nodded. "Yep, seen him around. Think he works for one of the small cattle outfits, not sure."

"He tried to bushwhack me," Spur said. " You know any reason he'd try that?"

The merchant squinted at Spur in the poor light of the coal oil lantern.

"You that Federal lawman." He shook his head. "Nope, don't know how he would be on either side in the city problems. Maybe he just don't like lawmen."

"Happens," Spur said. He stood and walked into the darkness leaving the dead man where he fell.

The saddlemaker was still working when Spur knocked on the locked front door. He sat on a chair beside a high table. Then Spur lost him. When the door opened Spur could still not see the Big Paul Smith he was looking for.

"Down here," Smith said. "Not everybody can be six-six."

Spur looked down and saw a perfectly formed small man, a midget no more than thirty-six inches tall. He stifled an urge to squat down to shake hands.

"Evening, Mr. Smith. My name is McCoy. Could we talk for a few minutes?"

Even in the dim light, Spur could see the man's eyes twinkle.

"Always glad to accommodate the United States Secret Service. I've been wondering how it can be secret if you told us who you are?"

"That seems to be the way with secrets. I'd like to talk to you for a few minutes if I could. Beth Johnson said I should come and see you."

"Beautiful Beth! Yes, a fine friend. Please come in." He closed the door and went back to his work bench, jumping up to a stool where he worked on a half done saddle.

Paul Smith was a true midget, his proportions were normal, he was simply a small man. His dark eyes showed an uncommon strength and understanding.

Dirk Fletcher

"Yes, the death of Harry Johnson. How does a perfectly healthy man one day, have stomach problems, and die overnight? It is an interesting question, and one I hope you are considering."

"Considering, yes. That's part of the reason I'm here. Do you have any special knowledge about this particular death?"

Smith punched a series of holes in a thick slab of leather, then began threading rawhide decoration through them. He shook his head slowly.

"Nothing in particular. But it does leave itself open to the question of foul play. Why or who, I would have no ideas."

"But you know the town."

"True, as well as anyone. I have more time to watch people, to assess them, to speculate, to evaluate. I'm an recalcitrant people watcher."

"And a well educated one."

"Mr. McCoy, I read a great deal."

"Who could cover up foul play in such a death?"

"You would need the doctor, the marshal and probably the undertaker."

"Let's start with the marshal. Why would he cover up a killing of a prominent, rich man?"

"I've thought about that. The why must be money, lots of money either now or in the future. Harry Johnson was the richest man in town. His father owned all the town at one time. He decided he wanted a community here and put up stores, and rented them, then sold them.

"Right now Beth Johnson owns about sixty percent of all the real estate property in Johnson Creek."

"And pays at least sixty percent of the taxes."

"True. I've eliminated all other reasons for homicide in Mr. Johnson's case. There is no woman

62

involved, no power struggle, no public image to maintain or shatter, no ambition to prove. That leaves only money for a motive. Find the money and you find the killer."

"If he was killed."

Paul Smith formed a piece of leather around the right side of the saddle and cut it to fit. "Mr. McCoy, we both know that Harry Johnson was murdered. We just don't know why." He smiled for a moment and then looked up.

"You see, I'm a good friend of the only undertaker in town. He told me certain curious facts that I'm sure Beth Johnson also knows. So we move on to motive and the 'who.' "

"Any ideas?"

"None whatsoever. First the motive, the money."

"What do you know about our ex-marshal?"

"A lot. Most of it not applicable to the current discussion. He went to war early, and came back quickly, wounded. In those days he was a strong willed man but weak in body. Now he has regained his physical strength, but he is a weak man, afraid of something. He's whole, but weak. I'm not sure why."

Spur watched the small man's strong hands tool a piece of leather, working in a pattern with awl, filed nail heads, and small hand tools.

"What's your views on the Carpetbaggers, Mr. Smith?"

"Opportunists, pure and simple. Half the people in town knows what the mayor's trying to do, they just don't know how to stop him."

"What is he trying, Mr. Smith?"

The small man smiled and his eyes went wide.

"To sack the city treasury. To rob Johnson Creek of every dollar he can get, then vanish to the north and leave the Negroes in the lurch without a friend, a dollar, a job, or a dole.''

"Just the way it has happened time and time again across the South since the Reconstruction laws," the Secret Service agent said. "The problem here is the timing. I'd need to catch him directly in the act."

"Timing is not a real problem for you, Mr. Secret Service man. Most money comes into a government entity when it levies taxes and those taxes are called due.''

"True." Spur laughed softly. "So tomorrow I can find out when the taxes assessments are due on city property."

"You don't have to wait. I have my statement, and I'll pay it on the last day. All taxes are due and payable in two days."

"Two days?"

"Day after tomorrow at 4 P.M. is the last moment to pay without a penalty. At least 95 percent of the taxes will have been paid by that last day."

"Mr. Smith, you don't give a man much time."

"Time is always on the side of the law," Smith said. He watched McCoy. "you're an educated man, college probably. Am I right?"

"Harvard. Economics."

Paul Smith put down his tools. "Well, well. This calls for an ivy hall celebration. I'm a Yale man. Do you have time for a serious meeting with a really good bottle of wine? It's from France and I've been saving it for a special occasion."

Spur grinned. "I'd be delighted, even to drink with a Yale man. Lead on McDuff!"

Smith lived in back of the wonderful leather smells of his shop. He led the way and Spur found himself in a finely decorated, and neatly kept living room. The furniture was half size, to accommodate Smith.

The small man waved Spur to a couch which was large enough for him. Smith pulled a bottle of wine from a wall rack and brushed dust off the label.

"Yes, yes! Almost fifteen years old! A rosé that I think you'll like." He pulled out the cork and sniffed it, then gave it to Spur.

"Aroma. One third of the test of a good wine. Body and taste, as I remember. But I usually only talk about wine when I'm drinking it, which may account for my fuzzy memory of wine and wines."

He poured two long stemmed wine glasses and passed the first to Spur. The Secret Service Agent had learned to like wine. They never had it at home in New York.

"A rosé, you say. I don't think I've tried it before."

"A man must try many things in his life to know what he likes. Like the winsome, beautiful Beth." He looked up sharply. "Don't laugh or I'll put you out of my house." For a moment he chuckled. "It might be a hard thing for me to do, even with a shotgun, but never mind. I was talking about the sweetest rose of any I know, Miss Johnson."

"You've had your eye on her for a time?"

"Aye, I have. And even in four years she has grown away from me. Once we were the same size." He took a deep breath that came as a sigh of resignation. "Some things just can't be helped. I would have given everything I own if she would have stopped growing when she was thirty-five inches tall."

"Yes, my friend, but remember the man who said: 'There is no wisdom in useless and hopeless sorrow.'"

"Games, I love games! Let's see, useless and hopeless sorrow. Sounds like Shakespeare, but it isn't. No . . . I almost had it. Yes . . . I have it, the letters. The letters of Samuel Johnson."

Spur laughed and clapped in appreciation. "Sir, not one man in ten thousand would know that quotation, least of all who had written it first. How come you do?"

Paul Smith smiled, sniffed of the wine, then drained the glass.

"Yes, the glories of praise. 'Man is wont for praise.' Who said that?"

"Shakespeare, Milton, perhaps Ben Franklin?"

"Wrong on all counts. That statement is by one Paul Smith, Esquire. At your service. How did I know the Sam Johnson quote? I was a master in English at Yale. I graduated second in my class secure knowing that I had a teaching position in a small private college in the East. We contacted each other by letter. My letters of recommendation were laudatory, and I was given assurances I had the position as lecturer in English Literature."

He filled his glass again. "Then as you suspect, I arrived on the campus. I was there for approximately twenty minutes before I was sent packing. It seems they had no place for a small man."

"A small man with a large mind was what frightened them," Spur said. "I shall never send any of my children to that school!"

"Nor I!" Paul shouted, then laughed. "And since neither of us have any children, at least any to speak of, 'tis an easy task, Horatio!"

Spur held up his wine glass and Paul filled it.

"Now to the rub. How now you and Shakespeare? Did this lout, this commoner, this toiler in the stable, this handyman around a theatre, really write the works attributed to one William S. or perchance was it the honorable Lord, the highborn and higher yet educated Sir Francis Bacon?"

"You fault me sir!" Paul cried. Then fell into a spate of laughing. "Must we continue to speak in Shakespearian quotes? Me thinks not!" He laughed again.

"While at Yale I made a close study of both men. And at last I came to one conclusion. Bacon was three years older than Willy. And Bacon lived about ten years longer than Shakespeare. While Bacon seemed the more logical man to write the Shakespearian plays with their wit and wisdom and their high tone and such a *feeling* of the English highborn, the man himself, Bacon, was not mentally capable of doing the task. Nor did Bacon know that much about theatre."

Spur raised the usual counter argument and settled down to an evening he hadn't enjoyed since leaving the ivy halls. It would be a good four hours before the argument, still long from resolved, was given up for the time, and Spur headed for his room at the hotel.

7

Don White had brooded about his situation ever since that lawman, that Spur McCoy, had left the City Hall. For a while he had retreated into his private quarters. Then he went out and ate the biggest steak dinner the hotel could offer. He felt somewhat better. Back in his room he yelled at the four Negroes who were his private guard force, told them to move about, to do something.

The four guards, all armed with sawed off double barreled shotguns, occupied a room just behind White's. He had built in four bunks for them, and kept two on duty with him around the clock on twelve hour shifts. Waking or sleeping, he was protected.

The City Hall had once been a store. He had refitted it, moved in the city jobs from several locations, and built himself quarters in back, all rent free of course, courtesy of the city.

His bedroom was large, eighteen feet square, with a big bed in one corner. It had been specially made for him and was twice as wide as most double beds. The bathtub in the other corner was special too, a lay down kind, with fancy claw legs.

He walked into the big room now and took off the jacket which he always wore. It separated him from the common folks in this hick town.

There was one other person in the room, a slender black girl with firm, full breasts and short hair. She now sat cross-legged on the big bed. She wore a skirt but nothing above her waist. She smiled and shook her shoulders so her breasts did a fancy and practiced little dance.

Her name was Ruth, and she had been a dance hall girl in Houston before he rescued her. She wouldn't say for sure, but he guessed that she was about twenty.

"Hey, our mayor is here! Your Honor, sir. You have a good supper?"

He stood in front of her staring down.

"Damn good. I deserved it. I'm keeping your belly full, ain't I?"

"Right now I'd rather you filled something else. You wanting? You ready? I can get you ready quick."

White ignored her, went to the back door and told one of the guards to move to the front door, outside it, and kept one man on the rear. There was no window in the big room. He called it his maximum secure position.

When the men were situated, he went back to the bed and sat down. Ruth curled around him from the back. She had slipped off her skirt and was naked black. She snaked under his arms, then up his chest and nibbled at his lips. Her breasts massaged his chest as she moved slowly from side to side, then lifted higher, pushing one breast then the other into his mouth.

White bit the morsels, teased her erect black

nipples, then roughly pushed her away. She landed on the bed, bounced and came up to her knees at once and walked toward him.

"Something different," he said. "Make it damn different. You used to be more fun."

Ruth sensed the threat. She knew she was temporary and could be replaced at any time. She came up behind him again, stripped off his shirt, then took down his pants and pulled his half boots off so he was naked white.

On the hard floor in front of where White sat on the bed, Ruth did a dance. It was basic and sexy. She had learned it from a black whore in New Orleans when she was sixteen. Ruth had never known the dance to fail to bring the man danced for into heat.

It began slow, her whole body not a foot in front of White, gyrating and swaying in motion to an African beat. Ruth heard the dance was a fertility rite and she had no doubts. It got her as worked up as it did the man.

She kept her body gyrating, moved her big breasts so they swayed and jiggled half an inch from his face. Then moving in so they brushed his lips and then away.

With each half a minute the beat quickened. Her hips swung and her black crotch hair glistened from her sweat. She came toward him again, her legs spread, jumping in little steps toward him, her crotch open, exposed, offered.

She nudged him with her shoulders and with her hands, eased him back on the bed. Ruth went to her knees on each side of his torso and slowly humping and grinding her hips, worked up higher and higher toward his face.

She saw the glints in his eyes, heard his breathing

surge faster. His long stick was hard and ready. She moved higher on his chest, closer, higher yet.

At last her hips reached a surging, grinding speed that brought a wail from White.

Her hips slowed and she positioned them directly over his face. A wet stream seeped down her right leg. Her outer lips were swollen and oozing.

Slowly she lowered herself over him. He cried out again in need and she let her labia settle over his face.

White jammed his tongue upward. For a minute he drank in her juices, then he slammed her to the bed, lifted her to her hands and knees and spread her legs. He bellowed in satisfaction as he took her from the rear.

She yelped in surprise and fulfillment as he slammed into her again and again.

"Take that you little black slut!" he roared. "You asked for it! Christ, how did you learn to fuck so good, so many ways? You must have had a damned good teacher."

Then he lost control and jolted against her so hard she crumpled to the bed as his one hundred and seventy pounds hit her with all the force he could manage.

A minute later he rolled to one side and lay on his stomach, his breath coming like fissures in a giant steam vent.

Ruth sat beside him combing her hair. She snorted softly and looked over at him.

"Was that different enough for you, Big Stud? You man enough to take that three times a day? You think you'll ever find a mama who can do you better? Not a chance. I'm your woman for now and for as long as time, or until I get knocked up. But that ain't ever gonna happen cause I know how to stop it. So you just rest up and when you're ready, I'll show you another way, something so wild you might just be knocked on your tail for a whole week!''

She laughed softly, went to the bathtub and poured in two buckets of hot water and had a luxurious bath, while Don White slept, trying to gain back some of his strength.

He came upright an hour later. The working day was not over yet in the city clerk's office outside. White dressed, ignored Ruth's naked black form, and went back into the City Hall section of the building.

One of the store owners stood before Victor, paying his taxes.

"Too damn much," the merchant said. "Just barely able to make a living as it is."

"Yeah, don't complain so much or I'll raise your taxes to double, you got that?" Victor said. The merchant gave him thirty-six dollars, took a receipt and stalked out of the room.

White had come in quietly, and stood in back of Victor, as the small Negro counted the money. He divided it in half, put half of it in the small strong box under his desk, and the rest in his pants pocket.

White didn't say a word. He opened the door into his quarters silently, then closed it smartly and walked toward Victor.

"Yes suh, Mistah White. We doing good business today. Take in one hell of a lot of money. You wanta count it?"

"Later, Victor. Time to close up. I'll help. Don't want you hurting your back carrying all that money." White picked up the portable strong box and motioned for Victor to follow him, and walked back to his private quarters.

He put the strong box on the bed, and nodded at it and then Ruth. She had not dressed. She posed for Victor who grinned and reached for her breasts. She edged away out of reach.

"Back here, Victor," White said. They went through the back guard room where two men slept and into an unused section of the old store behind that. Light came through a sky window.

White held out his hand. "Saw you shorting the county up there, Victor. Your black ass is in trouble."

"No suh, Mistah White! I just making it easier to count." His eyes went wide, then he backed up as White's big fist hit him in the side of the face. A bone broke, and Victor screamed. He jolted to one side and ran for the back door, but White beat him there.

White thundered a stiff right fist into Victor's unprotected belly. The black man bent over and White rammed his knee upward, slamming Victor's head high, disorienting him. He nearly fell, then staggered.

White took his time now, first his right fist, then his left smashed into Victor's battered face. When he bent low enough, White powered his knee upward into Victor's jaw. At last he fell down and couldn't get up.

White knelt beside him, picked up Victor's arm and held it.

"Victor, you just got fired. I never want to see your ugly black face again, you hear? I see you again, I'll have one of the guns put both barrels of double ought buck through your guts. You get out of town fast or you're dead meat!"

White slapped Victor's face gently.

"You understand, boy?"

Victor's head nodded slowly.

White caught the black arm again, held the wrist in one hand and Victor's elbow in the other. Then he slammed the forearm down across White's knee.

Victor screamed as both forearm bones broke and jagged bone daggered through the flesh becoming white streaks in the bloody red field.

White went through the unconscious man's pockets, took out a wad of greenbacks and ten double gold eagles. He put the money in his pants and kicked Victor in the ribs. Then picked up the still unconscious Victor and threw him out the back door into the alley.

Back in his bedroom he soaked his hand in a pan of cold water and scowled at Ruth.

"Get your damn clothes on. I don't want you running around here bare assed unless I tell you to. And keep your tits covered up too. This ain't some damn whore house. You want to peddle tail you wait until I'm through with you." He lifted his hand to slap at her rump, but she wiggled it out of his reach.

She dressed slowly, where he could watch.

"Just one more, it's early."

"Shut up, I got problems. I just had to send Victor on vacation. Now I need a new city clerk."

"I could to that. I can read and write and add."

"You'd have to leave your clothes on. Wouldn't work. I'll get somebody for tomorrow."

He opened the strong box on the bed, and Ruth jumped on top of the money.

"Glory! Look at all that cash money! I love it!"

He back handed her along the rump pushing her off the money. Quickly he separated the bills into denominations and counted them, then the double eagles. They had taken in a thousand, two hundred and twenty-seven dollars that day.

"That makes nearly five thousand, here and in the bank," White said as if thinking out loud.

"When we leaving, Big Stud? Tonight? Just you and me and the money the way you promised? We ditch these shit pitching blacks and let them make out the best they can?"

White looked at her, caught her arm and pulled her toward him. He played with her breasts through the fabric of her thin blouse.

"Not tonight. We can make another thousand dollars tomorrow. You know how much I worked for in Chicago? Twenty-five dollars a month! A thousand dollars is more than three years of pay for what I was doing! Three god damned years! You don't even know how much money a thousand is."

"Yes I do, honey. And I want me a diamond necklace just as soon as we hit Houston. You promised me. Remember, swore a fucking oath and you promised."

White sat there looking at her. He was seeing Emma Lou Fisher, back in Chicago. The sweet little girl who had let him touch her breasts just once, then told him if he wanted to do that again he had to marry her. She had been a tease, but he wanted her so damn bad.

He'd go back with his five thousand and he'd take her everywhere and buy her presents and clothes and show her off and get her so hot that she'd pull off her dress and the rest of her clothes the first time he asked her to. She was going to be a great new bedmate.

Yeah! This would all be worth it to see the expression on her face when he slammed his ten inches deep into her slot! She would love it, and with five thousand . . . he could set himself up in business. Just one more day. One more day!

8

Spur McCoy had been up and moving for three hours when the Needlecraft and Stitchery shop opened on Main Street. This small place, with its living quarters in back, was the workplace of June Black, the best seamstress in this half of Texas.

When she lifted the roll blind on the door, Spur McCoy crossed the street from the leaned back chair he had been holding down in front of the hardware, and went inside.

He wasn't ready for the attractive woman who looked up at him. She was black and she wasn't. She was Indian but something more. It was a delightful combination that Spur McCoy found immediately appealing.

"Good morning, and what can I do for you, Mr. Spur McCoy?"

White teeth flashed as she grinned, her dark eyes doing a little dance as she saw his surprise. Her face was oval, not round, with a firm jaw and high cheekbones. June's skin was a soft brownish shade, her hair jet black and cropped close around her head. Full eyebrows and dark bangs cut straight over her eyes, gave her a slightly wild look.

"One of the nice things about a small town," Spur said slowly. "Everyone knows everyone else, especially a stranger. You must be Miss June Black, the best seamstress in Texas."

June smiled, looked down at the seam she was stitching. Then she glanced up. "I probably am, but damn few will admit it. How about a pair of hand tailored dress shirts, or a new suit? I'm good at men's clothes, too."

"I would think you are. No, my wardrobe isn't that important in this job. But I could use some advice. Mind if I sit and jawbone a while as you work?"

"I'd be pleased, honored that a U.S. Secret Service agent thinks I have any secrets." She laughed. "Besides *those* secrets, I mean."

She stood and went to a bolt of cloth. Spur McCoy sucked in a quick breath. Her figure was outstanding. High, full breasts, with a tiny waist and solid woman hips. She was only an inch or two over five feet, but it was the most interesting sixty-two inches of body Spur McCoy could remember ever seeing.

She cut a length of cloth off the bolt with scissors and returned to her cutting board.

"So, secrets," she said staring at him honestly. "You've probably got a secret or two yourself. You ask the questions, and I'll try to answer. Oh, somebody probably told you that I'm a talker. I do talk, so don't expect yes or no answers."

"Suits me fine. I don't have any yes-no questions."

"First, so you won't be too embarrassed to ask, but want to know. It was my mother who was a Negro and my father who was the Indian, a rampaging Kiowa brave who my mother never saw again after he took her by force three times one night. That was outside of Amarillo a ways. My ma died when I was ten and I've made my own way since then."

"I'd say you got the best features from both your parents. You're a beautiful woman, dazzling. I'm impressed."

Her smile brightened and her eyes thanked him. He went on.

"First, any comments on the Bagger here in town?"

"A few hundred. This man White is using my people for his own ends. We all know that, but so far there's no legal way to stop him, and this is a small town where we don't just up and shoot down somebody just because he might be doing bad.

"And those poor blacks he brought in from Houston? They nothing but cotton pickers. Not one in fifty of them can read or write. They vote the way White tells them. They mostly sit around and drink and chase the white women and play cards.

"You know them boys get a handout from the city? For doing nothing. Human welfare, or something like that White calls it. I never heard of no such thing in my life.

"Damn! I work ten, twelve hours a day and I hardly take in as much as they get for doing nothing. Then one or two of them comes around at night wanting me to haul their ashes for the pleasure of doing a real black man!"

"Any ideas how the Carpetbagger episode here is going to end, June?"

"Yes, the way they all end. The Bagger takes off some day just before he's about to get shot. He grabs whatever he can, or he plans it and gets out of town with every dime in the city treasury. But it's hard because you can't arrest a man for what he's going to do. Then after he does it, he's out of the county before you know he's even gone.''

"June, you almost sound like a policeman." Spur smiled at her and she looked up from her stitching and smiled back. Then Spur found himself watching the line of cleavage that showed just over her blouse, and the surging breasts the cloth covered. He could see her nipples clearly pushing out the fabric farther.

She caught him looking at her breasts and laughed. "Spur, I don't mind you checking out my tits. You wouldn't be a normal man if you didn't." She nodded. "Lands sakes, I don't see a man as handsome and as well put together as you but once in an old possum's age. You look, I don't mind."

It was Spur's turn to laugh to cover up his embarrassment.

"I didn't mean to be rude, but the whole package is just fantastic. Now, back to work. You must have known Harry Johnson. What can you tell me about his death? Did you hear anything? What about rumors around town? Anyone bragging about killing him?"

"Land sakes, Spur McCoy, you know I can't tell you nothing like that I heard. I'm kind of like a doctor or a priest, privileged information. Anyway the paper says Harry died of natural causes. Stomach ulcer or something."

Spur stood and bent over her cutting board. He put his hands on the surface and stared at her hard.

"June Black, this is the United States Government asking you a question. I can get a court order if I have to. If you know anything about Harry Johnson's death, you are required to tell me right now."

"Oh, Lordy, but you are sexy when you get so angry and demanding." She stood and walked to the shelf of bolts of cloth, fingered one for a moment and came back.

"All right. I guess you're right. Nothing legal in my not talking, but just didn't seem right." She stopped and frowned. "Yes, it was after Harry died. One of the men I see . . . talk to now and then . . . is Zed Hiatt, our councilman." She laughed softly. "The stories I could tell you about him. His wife died about three years ago, and he came in the back way one night so nervous he acted like a forty-five year old virgin."

She got up and went to a small pot bellied wood burning stove at the side of the room.

"You want some tea? I usually have some tea about is time of day. Long as it don't get too hot to have a fire." She built a quick fire and put a pot on with precisely two cups of water, then stepped back and made sure the fire was burning.

"Zed is one of those 'needing' kind of men. He needs to crack his gonads every couple of weeks, but more important he needs to feel a little domination over someone or something. He's not vicious or mean. But sex seems to give him a dose of normal aggressiveness. I used to know a professor in Houston who told me all of these things. He was an interesting man."

She went back to the stove, checked the fire, then the hot water and put the tea strainer in the pot. Two minutes later she poured tea into two cups.

"You take anything in your tea?" she asked. When he shook his head she came back with the cups.

"One night he came in, maybe a week ago, and was so excited he could hardly wait to get undressed. He told me that he had actually had a climax without me. He had told me that after his wife died he tried to masturbate, but couldn't ever make it.

"At first he said he couldn't tell me about his lost load, but I teased him and played with him and said I wouldn't do any more unless he told me. At last he did.

"Zed, gentle, quiet, inept little Zed told me that he had cum in his pants one night. It took me an hour to get it out of him, and finally he whispered to me. He said he had shot a man, and the excitement, the thrill of it had made him shoot his cum all over his pants."

She sipped at the tea watching him over the cup's rim. "As soon as he told me that I dropped the subject. I don't want to get involved in somebody getting killed. But as I thought back, the only person in town who had died recently had been Harry Johnson. But since he died of natural causes . . ."

"He didn't. This is confidential, June. Tell no one. Harry Johnson was shot five times, by five different guns."

She frowned, took the needle and began stitching on a dress sleeve again.

"Shot five times? But with five different guns? Why for goodness sakes? If a man is dead . . ."

"That's what I'm trying to find out, June. Anything you can tell me might help."

"You think . . . then it's possible . . . I can't believe that soft little Zed would ever . . ." She stood and went to the front window. "He was excited, even telling me about it. I guess it's possible that Zed could have been one of the men who shot Harry. But I don't have any idea why."

"Beth heard an argument by a number of voices just before the shots. By the time she got there everyone was gone and her father was dead."

"Oh, my God! That poor girl! She's always been one of my favorites in town. I do dresses for her. Of course we're not what you'd call social equals. Zed . . . my God! It's hard to believe."

She came back and sat behind her cutting table again.

"June, with this as a foundation, is there anything else that you've heard or heard about, that might tie in with Harry Johnson's murder? Anything at all, no matter how slight?"

She stitched on the sleeve for a minute, then her black eyes looked up at him.

"My God! It could be . . ." She shook her head. "But that just couldn't be. Ain't reasonable." She frowned and at last looked at him again.

"Two nights ago Garth Ludlow stopped by to collect his 'license fee.' He figures I owe him something. He was busting to talk. Some men get that way when they get worked up. Anyway he talked for an hour and then he said he had something he really wanted to tell me that I wouldn't believe. He said I'd be amazed at the four other men in on the little affair. Four others. Five men. I don't know. It could have been a poker game, or a target practice bet. I don't know."

"But he was more excited about this than usual?"

"Oh, yes. Lots of times he drops in, and wham bang and he's out of here. He was in the war. Gets afraid sometimes over almost nothing. He's not a real strong man, emotionally. Never saw why he wanted to be town marshal. Course nothing much happens up here."

Spur turned his low crowned brown hat around

and around in his hands.

"Four other men . . . that would make five of them. Five shot Harry. Circumstantial evidence. But it's a pointing. I thought at first that the town marshal would have to be in on the cover-up. I never figured he could be one of the killers."

"Wouldn't Doc Greenly have to be one of them?"

"On the cover-up, maybe on the murder too. Going to be damn hard to prove unless we can get somebody to confess. From what you've said, Zed is probably the weakest of the three. I'll have to have a confidential talk with the jeweler. My watch has been running a little slow lately anyway."

June stood and caught his hand. "That is all I can help you with on the Harry Johnson problem. Nothing else fits. Now, I have a problem of my own I want you to help me with."

She went to the front door, locked it and put a closed sign on it, and led Spur into the back part of the store. It had been converted into living quarters. There was a small cooking stove, a heater, a single bed and dresser and a table and two chairs.

"Home," she said. She turned toward him, put her arms around him and stretched up and kissed his lips. She held the kiss for a long time and pushed her body firmly against his. When her lips escaped from his she sighed.

"Spur McCoy, I have this wild, furious itch to know what you look like naked."

Spur moved his hand down until it held one of her big breasts and he grinned at her. "June, I've been wondering the same thing about you. If you've got the time, I've got some scratching that should take care of your itch."

She smiled and unbuttoned his shirt and ran her hands over his chest, playing with the thatch of black hair there.

"I kill for a man with hair on his chest." She eased off his leather vest, then took his shirt off.

As she did, he was busy with the blouse that covered up her twin points of interest. Under the blouse was a soft cotton chemise and under that a binder that made her bosom look somewhat smaller than it actually was.

As the binder came off, Spur's eyes widened in awe. Twin mounds surged away from the restricting cloth. Heavy, thumb sized nipples were already gorged with hot blood and he could almost see them pulsating. Palm sized areolas, a shade of pink lighter than the dark pink nipples crowned the surging breasts.

"Fantastic!" Spur said with a note of reverence. He bent and kissed each nipple, then licked and kissed one breast, then the other one.

June had closed her eyes and stood with her feet well apart so she wouldn't topple over. She smiled with her eyes still shut. "Spur McCoy, you are a man who knows how to treat a woman right. I love that. Most men just think of themselves and their own urgent need."

"I like to enjoy myself on the way there," Spur said. "I always figure that you might want the same kind of pleasure."

She caught his hand and pulled him toward the bed. "I have the rest of the morning. The first time you can do me hard and fast. Don't even take your pants or your boots off!"

She dropped on the bed on her back, lifted her knees and the skirt fell around her waist.

"Get me out of those damned drawers, quick!"

Spur found the buttons and snaps, and soon had the cotton drawers with small pink ribbons on them loose enough to pull down. She urged him on and slid the garment off her feet. Her legs lifted again and parted.

"Now! Spur sweetheart, do me now!"

By the time Spur opened his fly her legs were resting on his shoulders. She was open and wanting. He moved in closer, then positioned himself and drove in with a hard thrust.

"Oh, Damn!" June shrieked. "Wonderful! Wonderful! So good!" Her hips pounded up at him. "Harder, sweetheart! I love it! You're so good! More, more!"

For just a moment, Spur marveled at this small sex machine, then he concentrated on his work and three strokes later he felt the woman under him coil and explode. Her whole body rattled and shook. She screamed, her voice rising to a high pitch and then trailing off into a wail and a long series that lasted three or four minutes.

Her passion excited Spur and he jolted faster until he could no longer hold the floodgates and he erupted into his own climax that tore the last breath from him and stiffened his whole body as he planted the seeds of the race deep inside this writhing body below him.

Slowly they both tapered off and after ten minutes they lay in each other's arms, side by side, still connected.

Her eyes came open lazily and she stared at him.

"In ten years, I've never made love so marvelously!"

"It was wonderful."

Her gaze held his. "I want you to stay right here all day. Can you do that? I want to make love to you all day and then all night. I want to get you so worn out you won't be able to lift off the bed to put your clothes on!"

"Fourteen times," Spur said.

"What?"

"Fourteen times, my record. Can you stand it that many times?"

June grinned and rubbed her breasts against his chest. "My own personal record is twenty-seven. But I don't really talk about it. I was young and crazy then."

"How old are you now?"

For a moment she frowned at him, then shrugged. "Twenty-four, is that too old?"

"Of course not."

"I started making my living on my back when I was thirteen. I mean it was the only way I had to survive." She kissed him. "Now this is just a kind of hobby. I missed it at first, the human contact, the compliments. Now I'm selective. Hell, I even get political. I'm nice to the men who can protect me and help me in my business."

"You prefer dressmaking?"

"Of course! I'm an artist with a needle and shears. My big tits don't help me a whit there. If I cut the pattern wrong, or stitch the seam crooked, it shows, no matter how good my tail meets up with yours."

She pulled away from him, leaned in and kissed his nose. "You hungry? It's getting on toward midmorning. They say the young ones get hungry afterwards, and the older men get sleepy."

"I'm hungry," Spur said and laughed.

She made pan fried potatoes and onions for him. Slices of fresh potatoes fried in bacon grease and the onions put in the last two minutes. She had made bread the day before. It was sturdy and high without holes. June took fresh butter from a small square wooden box in one corner of the room.

"Look at this," she said. "The hardware store

man sold it to me. It's called an ice refrigerator, and I have ice brought in twice a week from the ice house. I can keep milk and meat and butter for three or four days without them spoiling."

"What won't they think of next?"

"I hear in New York a man is working on a horseless carriage."

"I've seen lots of those. The trouble is they can't move."

"This one can. It has a little motor on it, an engine of some kind, not steam, but something that runs on coal oil or such and chugs right down the road."

"I'll believe it when I see it," Spur said and dug into another helping of fried potatoes and onions. This time June added three fried eggs sunnyside up and some strawberry jam for the bread. She said she had made the jam herself.

It was just before noon when Spur dressed and walked to the rear door of the dress shop. June reached up and kissed his lips then stepped back.

"You stay away from me now, Spur McCoy. You'll ruin me for these local boys. It was a marvelous party." She frowned. "If I hear anything else about shootings that might tie to Harry, I'll certainly let you know about it."

She stepped back, then came forward and kissed him again.

"Oh, damn, what am I doing letting you get away?" She lifted her brows. "Being smart, that's what. I could never rope and hold a critter like you, Spur McCoy. Just don't forget me." She pushed him out the door and he heard her throw the bolt behind him.

Then she laughed softly, "Good bye, Spur McCoy, the best one ever!"

9

Spur walked down Main Street with a near martial beat as he headed for the jewelry store. He checked his pockets and found that his watch was not in its usual spot. He would have to go back to the hotel to pick it up before he went to see Zed Hiatt. The call had to at least appear to be legitimate.

He reversed himself for a block, and went up the hotel steps. The town was about the same, people still nervous, unhappy, now angry about the new tax increase.

Spur went into the Johnson House Hotel and asked at the small desk for his key. There was a note. Spur read it and looked around the small lobby. A woman on the far side facing the desk rose slowly and came toward him.

She was sturdy, with proper shoes, a skirt that brushed the floor and a proper jacket and hat even though the temperature was climbing into the eighties.

The note said simply: "Mr. McCoy. My name is Mrs. Walter Trembolt. Could I have a word with you over here? I'm a respectable woman. My husband runs the blacksmith shop and we are both good Baptists."

Spur smiled as the woman walked up to him.

"Mrs. Trembolt, I would guess."

She nodded curtly. "Yes, we must talk."

"We can talk right here in the lobby if that would be all right. Won't you sit down?"

She sat across from him in an upholstered chair. She was a woman of about forty, her face pinched as if from constant frowning. She carried herself stiffly erect and cold blue eyes now stared at him.

"Mr. McCoy, I understand you're a Secret Service agent from the Washington D.C. government. I don't know exactly what that is or what you're supposed to do, but you must help us."

"That's what I'm here for, Ma'am."

"This Mr. White from Chicago is an agent of the devil. You must drive him out of town and let us get back to our proper ways and go about our business of spreading the Good News about Jesus Christ our Lord."

"Mrs. Trembolt. I've been making certain inquiries about Mr. White. So far your local people have been able to find nothing he has done which is illegal. According to the Reconstruction Laws, there are certain changes that must come to the state of Texas. It's simply the law."

"The man is Lucifer incarnate! He is the devil himself and he is ruining our small community. I keep praying for God almighty to strike Don White dead, but I must not be praying hard enough."

"I'm sorry, Mrs. Trembolt, prayer isn't my line of work. What I deal with are legal facts showing that Mr. White has violated the law, any law. That way he can be tried, convicted and removed from office. Do you have any evidence I can use to do this?"

"Oh, no. I'm not one to go to the law. I'm a Christian. This man is violating our Christian principles and I want him removed from office."

"Mrs. Trembolt, I'm sure you're a dedicated Christian woman, but what we must have are facts, evidence."

The woman sitting across from him stiffened even more if that were possible. She sniffed.

"Mr. McCoy. I'll have you know I am the mother of four sons and three daughters. That is how *dedicated a Christian I am!* I'm doing my bit to populate this God-forsaken, wicked country with good Christian folks. I also try to do what is best for the community and the church.

"Surely this man can be reasoned with. No matter how anti-Christ, he must have some decency."

"Yes, Mrs. Trembolt it is possible. Why don't you go over to City Hall right now and reason with Mr. White? I'm sure he would be pleased to see you and have a long talk. I spoke with him only yesterday."

"Don't patronize me, Mr. McCoy. I am a responsible citizen, a loyal American, and I hate what this riffraff, this white trash from Chicago is doing to Johnson Creek!" She stood quickly, started to leave, then remembering her manners and turned back. Spur had stood as she did, she seemed surprised to see him standing. "Oh, well, good bye, Mr. McCoy. We must all work in our own ways for the glory of the Lord." She turned and began to walk away.

"Good bye, Mrs. Trembolt. I wish you every success," Spur said as she turned.

He watched her go with a small shake of his head. If only it were that easy. He was on his way up to his room when he was handed another note by the desk clerk.

"Sorry, Mr. McCoy, this one came earlier and I forgot it."

He opened the second note. It was from Beth: "Spur. Please come to my house for dinner and to stay here while you are in Johnson Corner. I have a large house as you know, and you can pick a room with a lock on the inside! I promise not to attack you. Hope to see you for supper tonight."

He smiled and pushed the note into his pocket, picked up his railroad type pocket watch from his room and headed toward the jewelry store. The doctor's office came into view first, so he made a short detour across the street.

Doctor Greenly had a modest practice. He was the only doctor in town and for fifteen miles on all sides. He lived in a house beside the converted store where he had his offices. The building had been painted white with a soft blue trim, and even looked clean on the outside.

He went in the door marked "Office" and was met by a smiling young woman who asked his name and what he wanted to see the doctor about.

"Miss, it's personal," Spur said after signing the sheet of paper pasted to a piece of cardboard.

The girl smiled. She seemed to be seventeen or eighteen.

"Mr. McCoy," she said glancing at the sheet. "Most medical work is highly personal. Is this medically personal or something else?"

"It's about a gunshot wound."

The girl glanced at him quickly. "You have a gunshot wound?"

"No."

"Oh!" She frowned and left the small waiting room at once. Spur saw two others in the room, one a woman with a baby, and the second an old man with one eye. McCoy sat on a wooden chair that had been painted the same light blue of the exterior trim. Must have had some paint left over.

A moment later the young girl came up to Spur. "Dr. Greenly will see you now," she said. "This way, please."

She led him into the next room, through it and down a hall to an office with a desk, two chairs, books and a framed medical degree on the wall.

Dr. Horace Greenly sat behind the desk looking at a yellow pad and a medical book, going from one to the other. He mumbled something, made a penciled note on the yellow sheet and frowned. When he looked up at Spur, the same frown was in place. The girl had left and closed the door.

"Gunshot wound?" he said staring at Spur. The doctor was in his late forties, short even for 1869 at five feet four inches. He had a full head of red hair which had lost none of its carrot color. His eyes were an emerald shade of green, and his face was pale, with bags under his eyes and a touch of whiteness creeping over the lens of his eyes. The "white blindness" could overwhelm him within ten years and he was fighting it.

He shook his head. "I'm afraid I don't understand. Who are you, and what's this about a gunshot?"

"My name is Spur McCoy, Dr. Greenly. The man who was shot is Harry Johnson. Harry was shot five times, by five different guns. How come you covered up a murder?"

Dr. Greenly was not surprised or shaken. He picked up his pencil and began making marks on the yellow papaer.

"As soon as I got there I knew Harry had been killed. Didn't see any sense in letting this town blow apart. I told his daughter, Beth, that the Carpet-baggers would blame the towners, and the towners would blame the Baggers. They'd start shooting up the town, we'd have the Civil War all over again. I didn't think it was worth it."

"So you lied."

"For a good reason. I reported it to the town marshal as a death by gunshot wounds by person unknown. We can open the investigation anytime when the town is quieted down."

"When is that going to be, Doctor Greenly?"

"I don't know, not for a while yet. Feelings still running high. You've been on the street."

'Do you have any ideas about who the killers could be?"

"None at all. I know there were five bullet wounds in and around the chest and heart. Beyond that it's out of my area. I'm a doctor, not a Pinkerton detective." He paused. "You are, though. Not Pinkerton, but with the U.S. Secret Service. This why you're in town, to look into a murder?"

"Partly. We received a letter from Harry Johnson saying he had something he wanted to tell us. He said he could tell the local authorities, but he didn't trust them."

"He was right about that. Bunch of damn Carpet-bagging bastards!"

"Well, Doctor, I'm glad to see that you're so calm and collected about this governmental problem the town has. I still am not satisfied with why you covered up a murder. Especially one that must involve five people."

"I told you my reasons. So arrest me. I told the lawman, so I don't think I broke any law."

"How about conspiracy to commit a felony? That's what covering up a murder is."

"Wouldn't make it to court in our county."

"It would in the Federal Court in Houston."

"We're a long way from Houston."

"Which of the five bullets killed Harry?"

"Can't say unless you can tell me which one was fired first through fifth. Two hit his heart, three in his lungs. Either of the heart shots would have done it. The lung punctures would have killed him, too, but slower."

"Dr. Greenly, I'm not at all pleased with your medical ethics in this case. Legally you're still liable to be arrested. If you discover anything else, anything at all, that touches on this death, you better look me up and tell me before the sun goes down on that day."

"Don't rightly know what that might be, McCoy."

Spur stood, his hat in his left hand. The doctor made no move to get up.

"Greenly, I hope your medical knowledge and skills are a lot better than your ethics." He walked out of the room without saying goodbye.

Outside in the street, Spur stared back at the neatly painted doctor's office. Something was still wrong here, but he had no idea what it was.

So the town marshal knew about the five bullets. Two people knew and did nothing. What would the marshal have to gain? The water was getting danker and murkier by the moment.

He turned and walked on toward the jeweler. The front door was open and he went in. The usual glass topped case showed fancy pocket watches, pendant watches and a collection of wedding rings and a few special pearl and diamond rings, bracelets and necklaces.

A tall, heavy man lifted a jeweler's glass from his eye and looked at Spur. He had to wait a moment for his eyes to readjust, then his smile seemed to slip off his face.

"Yes sir, how may I help you?" Zed Hiatt asked.

"Mr. Hiatt?" Spur asked.

"The same."

"Good, they tell me you're the best man in town on a good pocket watch. Mine seems to be running a mite slow lately."

"Probably needs cleaning."

"Don't have that much time. That takes a couple of days, doesn't it?"

"Would now, I have some ahead of you."

"Oh! Could you adjust it to run just a little faster? Isn't there an adjustment inside somewhere?"

"Yep, I can do that." Zed looked up at him. "You're that Secret Service man I heard was in town?"

"The same. I hear you're on the city council now."

"True, for all the good it does. Get outvoted three to one on every issue. Try to do things need doing. The coloreds only want to talk about money, the damn dole!"

"That upsets you, Mr. Hiatt?"

"Like it does every other white man in town. We should be thinking about gas lights for the streets, maybe some cobblestone or paving of some kind for Main Street. We don't, not now."

"Mr. Hiatt, what do you know about the murder of Harry Johnson?"

Zed had been opening the back of Spur's pocket watch. He dropped it on the workbench. His hands shook so hard he could not even hold the small jeweler's tool. Sweat beaded rapidly on his forehead. He looked up and fear oozed from his eyes.

"M . . . Murder? Heard he died of stomach problems."

"True, Zed, five lead slugs fired at close range from five different pistols, probably by five different people."

"The paper said . . . Murder? I don't understand." His voice had changed. It vibrated, he coughed once, his eyes watered. "I . . . He was a good friend. Known Harry a long time. Didn't know what you said. Five? Why would five people shoot . . . Oh, God! You sure you're right?"

"Positively. I'm in town to dig out the killers. Right now everyone in Johnson Creek is a suspect. Where were you that night about two weeks ago when Harry Johnson was murdered in cold blood?"

"Where? Two weeks ago? What night? Most likely I was home reading. I do lots of reading since Etta died." He started to get up, then changed his mind and almost fell off the chair as he eased back down.

"What the hell! I was probably home. How can a person prove he was home alone reading?"

"Tough thing to prove, Zed. Just wondered. You put some thought on it and try to come up with some witnesses. Maybe you played poker or went out for a drink, or had company. You think on it and I'll stop by later on this week. I have a lot of people to talk to."

Spur stood there for a moment.

"My watch?"

Zed seemed to come alive again. "Oh, yes." He picked up the watch, made a small adjustment on the inside and pressed the parts back together. "That should speed it up just a mite."

"How much do I owe you?"

"Never make charges for adjustments." He shook

his head. "Old Harry murdered. Just can't believe it."

"Going to surprise a lot of folks. Thanks for your help." Spur walked out and across the street where he went into the Overbay General Store and from the darker interior, watched the jeweler's office.

Spur had investigated a pair of fine leather riding gloves for only a moment when Zed came out of his shop, locked his door and walked quickly up the street. Spur waited until he was half a block ahead, then followed on the other side of the street.

Another half block down, Zed turned into the *Johnson Creek Record* office. Spur stepped into a saloon and bought a beer and watched through the front window. Curious. Had he frightened the big man? He had been surprised when Spur used the word, murder. Dropped Spur's watch and his tool.

An over reaction even for a friend of Harry's. Yes, this and what June had told him seemed to point to Zed Hiatt as one of the five killers. But why? He could see nothing in common for the three men he suspected so far. They all lived in the same town, that was about it.

Scare a calf and it ran for its mother. Frighten a child and it often ran home or to a parent. Scare a killer, wouldn't he run for support to someone else who had also been in on the plot? That could mean that Hans Runner, the newspaperman was also in on the plot. He certainly didn't tell the right story in his paper.

June said that Garth Ludlow had been excited about something a week ago, but changed his mind and wouldn't tell her. It could tie in. He would be a more sure fourth suspect now. He knew about the five slugs in the dead man, but had not mentioned it. Was he the fourth man who pulled a trigger that night? Maybe he was painting Dr. Greenly with the wrong brush. Perhaps he *was concerned* about the town. He might not be involved.

But why had five men who knew Harry Johnson murdered him?

He needed to have some idea why these men banded together in the first place. What held three or four such different types together? He could not figure out anything they had in common.

After a half hour had passed and Zed had not left the printing plant, Spur walked over and tried the door. Locked. He saw a note on the front door. It said "Out . . . Be Back SOON."

Spur pondered that a moment as he walked away. Two killers could be going to talk to the other three. He would be especially careful with his back from now on. No open windows, no dark alleys, no light in his room.

There were five men in town with each one thinking he was a killer. In this case Spur hoped that thinking did not make it so . . . again with him as the victim.

10

Spur had walked only half a block away from the newspaper office when he heard a shot. His hand darted to his hogleg and came up with iron.

A buggy had just turned the corner a hundred feet ahead of him and headed away from him down Main Street. He could see four black men in the rig, each with a rifle, shotgun or pistol. They shouted and screamed and fired their weapons at second story windows as the horse and buggy raced down Main.

Spur was too far away to stop it. He could only watch as the rig tore along Main, scattering horses, other rigs and pedestrians as the Negroes blasted windows. Half the glass in the second and third floor of the Johnson House fell to the onslaught.

As quickly as it began the shooting stopped and the rig turned off Main and was gone. Half a dozen men jumped on horses and spurred after the four men. It was doubtful they would ever find the right ones.

Spur walked toward the small marshal's office. Were the shootings the result of a plan, or was it just four liquored up men with nothing to do?

Three stores ahead of him more firing sounded. Two shots blasted into the Texas afternoon. Spur raced forward, saw two cowboys duck and run away from an empty store next to the freight office. Another shot blazed into the stillness. Now Spur knew it came from the empty store.

Inside the store someone screamed, then Milicent Trembolt staggered out of the unused store. Her skirt was half ripped off and bloody. Her blouse hung on her shoulders in shreds where it had been sliced twenty times by a sharp knife. Both her breasts showed plainly through the tatters. Blood stained one breast.

She held a six-gun in both hands, swung around and fired it again into the store. A Negro man tumbled out of the doorway, his shirt off, one hand holding his bloody shoulder.

Before anyone could move, Mrs. Trembolt lifted the weapon and fired from six feet away, hitting the black man in the face, slamming him backward into a quick death.

Mrs. Trembolt screamed and dropped the gun. Two women rushed forward and caught her just before she fell. The women quickly covered her and helped her walk slowly into the drug store next to the freight office on the other side.

Doc Greenly hurried up the boardwalk and into the store. Spur checked the body of the colored. He was dead. There were signs of a struggle and blood in the old store.

Spur stood in the doorway of the drug store. Doc had the woman sitting up and he was talking to her. A moment later he urged her to stand and they went out through the alley toward the doctor's office.

Spur looked up as someone screamed as he ran forward. The sound came from a large man with a bare

100

chest and arms like oak branches. He waved a double barreled shotgun in his right hand.

"Oh, God! Here comes Walt!" someone said.

"He finds out what happened to his wife he'll gun down every black man he can find!" another voice said.

Spur stood on the boardwalk between the raging man and the store where his wife had been. Walt charged forward, started to brush past Spur. Too late he saw the foot out. Spur tripped Walt and grabbed the shotgun as Walt stumbled past him and then sprawled in the dust.

Spur broke open the weapon, let both shells fall into his hand and closed it again.

Walt began to get up.

"Hold it, Walt!" Spur commanded in his best parade ground voice. The talk around the boardwalk stopped. Walt looked up, his face a furious mask of hatred.

"Black bastards hurt my wife! I got a right to kill them!"

"Which ones, Walt? How you going to know which ones? You kill anybody, Walt, and I'll throw you in your own iron jail. You want that?"

Walt roared with rage and crawled to his hands and knees. Spur kicked him in the stomach just hard enough to roll him over and knock half the wind out of him.

"Stay down, Walt, or I'll have to lock you up. Do you want that?"

Walt sat up sucking in air. When he could talk he shook his head. "Where's my wife?"

"Over at Doc Greenly's," Spur said. "Why don't you walk on over there and help her? She needs you now."

Walt stood slowly, nodded at Spur and reached

for his long gun.

"I'll keep it for a while, Walt. It'll be down at the marshal's office. Pick it up tomorrow."

Walt nodded and walked off toward the doctor's office.

Spur turned and strode across the street toward City Hall. The Secret Agent pushed open the door and walked inside, saw the mayor's office door closed and marched up to it. He turned the knob and rammed the door open so hard it hit the wall.

Mayor White had his feet up on the desk as he worked out some final plans. He sat up quickly when Spur leaned over his desk.

"Take it easy, McCoy. We've had enough problems around here for one day. I know, I know. I heard all about it. None of my doings. Those men are citizens, free to get in trouble or not just like any other citizen."

"Bullshit!" Spur McCoy roared. "We both know what those men are, and how you got elected. You've got an hour to get out of here, to take your black voters out of town, at least two or three miles and set up a camp."

"Not likely. You've got no authority."

Spur drew the .44 off his hip so fast White suddenly was staring down the black muzzle of death. Spur pressed the iron's cold barrel against White's forehead.

"As I was saying, Mayor White. You get your men out of here within an hour. This is a forced evacuation for the public good and you will obey. If you don't, half of them could be shot down in a blood bath. If you thought the town was on edge before, you haven't even started to know what it's like out there now.

"You get out the back way with your people, NOW!"

"Impossible, McCoy."

Spur holstered the weapon in one smooth move, caught White by the shirt front and one arm and threw him against the wall. White hit and sagged, slumping to the floor, total surprise washing over his face.

"Right now, damnit!" Spur thundered. "Do you get the picture? Do you finally understand the danger?"

"Yes, yes. All right. I'll get things started. This is just temporary."

Spur spun around and ran back to the street.

Garth Ludlow stood there moving people past the death scene. He wore his marshal's badge again. He waved Spur over.

"Figured it was about time I came back to work. Looks like the town can use me."

"That's for damn sure."

"Oh, Father Desmond is looking for you. Any idea what he wants?"

"Personal, Marshal. Something personal." Just then the priest came through the crowd and called to Spur. The Secret Agent walked to meet the priest in his black habit.

"Mr. McCoy, I'd like to talk to you. There's something I need to tell you."

"Father it will have to wait. Right now we have a near riot shaping up. I'd appreciate it if you could stay visible here on the street and try to calm down the people you have some influence with. It would be a help."

"Yes, of course. I'll be glad to help. Could we set up a meeting first thing in the morning? Things should be settled down by then."

"That will be fine, Father. About nine o'clock."

Spur heard screams up the street and he moved that way. By the time he got there things had quieted down. He was afraid the rest of the afternoon was going to be like that.

It was. People grouped on the street talking about what to do to the coloreds. Then word came through that the Negroes had all moved out, they went south somewhere.

"Hail, I don't know if they coming back or not," one cowboy said. "I saw a whole bunch of them riding and walking down the Amarillo road, about an hour ago."

"Let's go after them!" Somebody shouted.

Spur fired the borrowed shotgun into the air and quickly broke up the budding riot.

Twice more before dark he used the shotgun to get the attention of troublemakers. It was a miracle that nobody got killed.

He slipped up the steps to his second floor hotel room and found it was one of those that had had windows blasted out. A light burned in his room when he got there and he pushed the door open with the muzzle of his .44.

Beth Johnson sat on the bed playing solitaire with a new deck of cards. She had swept up the glass and shaken it all out of the bedding.

"Hi," Beth said. "You've been busy."

"Just another day as a glamorous Secret Service agent," Spur said slipping the lock on the door and pushing a chair under the handle. He dropped his gunbelt over the bedpost and sat down beside her.

"You get my note?"

"Yes. Been busy."

"So I've heard. Are we worth it?"

"Some of you."

"Good. I figured you were not going to come up to my house so I decided to come to yours. You haven't had dinner yet so we have fried chicken, biscuits and gravy, mashed potatoes, three vegetables and sliced peaches for dessert. Hungry?"

He ate everything she brought. It was long past dark when he finished the last of the food and the two bottles of warm beer. She explained they had been cold when she brought them.

"Any progress on my father's five killers?" Beth asked.

"I think I may know who four of them are, but I still have no idea why, or what binds these men together in this kind of an execution plot."

She sat on the edge of the bed, her pretty face in a frown, brown hair sweeping over her shoulders. "I know Daddy went to play poker once a month or so. Would that help? He never liked to play much but said it was a get together for old times sake."

"Who did he play with?"

"I don't know. He never said. I never thought it was important enough to ask. I don't even know where he played."

"Not at one of the saloons?"

"No, it must have been at somebody's house. He mentioned once or twice that the man's wife really had a good snack for them after the game."

"One more question. Does the city have an account at your bank?"

"Yes, three or four of them. Why?"

"Make some excuse and don't let them take out any money from any of the accounts. Special bank examiner is coming or something."

"Why? It's city money."

"But the wrong people may draw it out and keep

it, like stealing, like Carpetbaggers."

"Oh. I don't know, it might be worth it to let him take the money and leave. Then most of the coloreds would leave too, because the dole would end fast. Maybe a few of the good workers would stay."

"Tomorrow, he'll try to make his run tomorrow. I made him get all of his blacks out of town so they wouldn't get massacred." Spur slid down on the bed and closed his eyes.

"Hey, you can't go to sleep. I know I promised not to seduce you, but that doesn't mean you can't at least kiss me once, or twice, or a dozen or more."

Spur laughed and pulled her down beside him. He kissed her and she snuggled against him.

"That's better. I hate a man who is a hard loser."

"Who lost? I thought I was winning. I have this winsome wench in my bed and the door's locked. I've just had a great meal she brought and she has no one to protect her honor."

Beth giggled. "Now we're starting to get somewhere."

"Be quiet and kiss me."

She rolled over on top of him and giggled.

"What's so funny?" he asked.

"I was just wishing that I had huge tits like June has so I could pop one out about now and slowly lower the dangling beauty into your mouth."

"Size isn't everything. Let me show you what I mean." He opened the buttons on her dress, pulled up her chemise and lowered her right breast into his mouth. He kissed the breast, then licked the nipple until she squealed, then sucked her whole breast into his mouth.

"Yes, yes! I think you might have a wonderful idea there. Who needs cow tits!"

Beth moaned softly. "My God but that makes me

hot! How do you get me worked up so fast!'' She reached for his crotch and found a growing lump there. Eagerly she massaged it and it grew in size.

He shifted to her other breast.

"I feel so warm all over, so soft and wanting. I feel like my breasts are on fire and my . . . my down there . . . is all soft and wet!''

She pulled her breast from his mouth and sat up. Quickly she opened his belt and then his fly and tugged his pants and short drawers down. His manhood leaped up eager for combat.

"Oh my! He's so huge! I didn't know they ever got that big. I mean the only other time . . . well he was just a kid really. My God, look at him!''

Her hands closed around his shaft and held him tenderly. She touched the purple head and moaned softly. Then her hands lifted his heavy scrotum and played with his balls.

When she leaned over him there were tears in her eyes.

"Spur I want you to take me so much, but it wouldn't work. It hurt the first time, and I know . . . I just know that nothing that huge would ever fit inside me. If it did it would hurt so much I'd die!''

"All your big talk was just talk, wasn't it? There isn't a man's prick made that won't fit in any grown woman. It just takes some warming up, some getting ready. I promise it won't hurt. Christ you've got me so wanting you now . . .''

"Won't hurt?''

"It will feel so good you'll die of pleasure.''

As he talked he massaged her breasts. He saw the small nipples rise and fill with blood. Then he ran his hand down her stomach to the top of the skirt.

"I really shouldn't.''

"But you want to.''

"Yes, so much, and with you! Only with you forever!"

"That's a hell of a long time."

"Good."

He slid his hand under the waist of her skirt and she caught it for a moment. He kissed her lips and she sighed and released his hand.

"I . . . I guess maybe . . ."

His hands found the fasteners at the side and he opened them, then pushed her skirt down. She wore two petticoats. He pushed them down too, then pulled her skirt and petticoats off over her feet.

Gently he took off her shoes and began massaging her feet.

"What are you doing?"

"Part of that getting ready. Do you like this?"

"Yes, it's relaxing."

His hands left her feet and worked up her gently curved legs. He marveled how fresh and pure they were, unmarked by bruise or cut or age.

When he came to her undergarment, it was a short kind of frilly silk he hadn't seen before. It had elastic around the waist and around each leg. Gently he pushed his hand under the elastic and down her tender, flat belly.

"Oh, no!" she said sharply. Her hands pressed on his hand through the fabric.

Again he kissed her, forcing his tongue between her teeth and into her mouth. Beth sighed softly, her hand came away and he moved it lower as the kiss continued.

He found the thatch of soft hair and stroked it. She murmured something, then sighed and he felt her legs drifting apart.

Quickly he bent and put his head to her crotch and before she noticed, he chewed a hole through the soft silk fabric. She half sat up and watched him fascinated.

"That's the most outrageous, the sexiest thing I've ever heard of!" she said half in awe, half in desire.

"Now, sweet Spur! Do me now! Push him into me!"

But Spur wasn't ready. His hand went to the hole in the silk and he stroked her outer lips, rubbed her tiny clit again and again until she screamed in joy and jolted in a gyrating, bouncing climax that left Spur in stark wonder. When she quieted she looked up at him.

"Maybe now, I'm ready?"

He nodded. She smiled, grabbed his penis and pulled it toward her crotch.

Spur lowered and nudged her slit. The lips parted and juices flowed and a second later he slid into her depths without a flicker of fear or pain from Beth.

"It's . . . it's . . . indescribable!" she said at last.

He made it last, coming almost to his climax, then pausing and backing away. Three more times Beth climaxed as he carried her along. Then in one tremendous rush they both came at the same time and lay there panting, her slender flanks heaving, his chest pounding to gain more air.

Her arms wrapped around him like a barbed wire fence.

"Now I'll never let you go," she said. "Anybody else would be a let down."

"Almost every man and woman is good in bed."

"Not like this. I have an idea. I have plenty of money. Why don't we get married and we can . . . can fuck this way every night for a hundred years!"

Spur shook his head and kissed her nose. "I'm not the marrying kind, at least not right now."

"Then don't marry me, we'll live in sin and we can make love this way every night for fifty years!"

"Fifty years is a long, long time."

Beth pouted for a minute. Her brown eyes shadowed with petulance. She swung her hair around so it covered his face.

"At least you can stay here and do it to me every night for two years, or until I get so sore I can't even spread my legs!"

He kissed her again.

"We'll talk about it," he said and a short time later they both went to sleep.

She woke him before morning and had him ready. They made love again. It had been the greatest night of her life and Beth didn't want to let it end. But her eyes turned heavy and she gave in at last and slept.

11

When Father Desmond talked to the Secret Service Agent Spur McCoy, he had made up his mind what he must do. He had to tell someone about the whole thing. He had struggled with the burden for too long. It had been a lark for him at first, a kind of rebellion, a release perhaps.

Then after the first shots had been fired, a course was set that no one, not even God could change. He thought about that for a moment and quickly changed 'could' to 'would.' All of the death, the screaming, and then . . . the find.

Father Desmond shook his head. He stayed on the street for an hour, talking to people, trying to calm them down. He decided he had been at least partly successful. There were no more shootings and very few squabbles.

He had urged all his Catholics to go home and leave the situation to the authorities. He had done little enough. Even if he had helped save one person's life this afternoon, he was still far, far from making up for that terrible night four years ago.

Pushing it all far away into the back alleys of his

mind, he headed toward the church and his quarters. He slipped in without Calida hearing him, went straight to the small chapel he had built in one of the rooms, and prayed on his knees for half an hour. Then he prostrated himself on the floor in front of the crucified Christ and prayed without ceasing for an hour.

Only then could he get to his feet and go into the living room, where Calida waited for him. She was such a pure vessel, so uncomplicated, uneducated, and trusting. Tonight he told the cook to go to her relatives house for a visit. Then he and Calida made their own supper in the big kitchen.

He had exactly what he wanted: a vegetable stew with just a few pieces of browned beef thrown in to give it flavor. He seasoned it with a whole bay leaf and let it cook its flavor through the mixture. He added enough water so there would be a juicy gravy to cover the potatoes when mashed on his plate.

For years, cooking had been one of his vices. He gave it up one year for Lent as he remembered, and somehow never found the time again.

Calida smiled at him as they worked on the food. She unbuttoned the simple white blouse she wore saying that it was too warm. She wore nothing under it, and the open blouse offered many quick glimpses of her breasts. Father Desmond was stirred, sexually, as he had been so many times lately.

After the meal, they left the dishes for the cook to wash the next day and retreated into his study and bedroom. Once inside Calida locked the door and stripped off her blouse.

She walked slowly to him, her arms out, her breasts swaying delightfully.

Father Desmond cursed himself silently. He had

hoped to be strong enough this one last time, but there was no chance. She needed him! He nearly laughed out loud at his justification. A thirteen year old girl does not need sexual gratification. She hardly understood his passion, and so far had shown none of her own.

He caught her hand and pulled her to the floor. Slowly he kissed her body from the top of her head down to her toes, casting aside any shielding clothing in the process. She lay on the bare floor looking at him, her eyes trusting, her lips curved in a sweet smile.

How had he come to this point? How had a man of God become a whiskey priest and a priestly seducer?

Even as he thought of it, he wasn't sure. His very first sexual experience had been with another altar boy. The other boy had been nearly thirteen and he asked Desmond if he'd ever jerked off. Desmond was twelve and he had heard the words, and knew what they meant, but hadn't tried it.

Once when climbing a tree he had strained to get to a limb and he felt his penis harden and something jet out of it. But he had never tried to make it happen.

They sat down behind the altar after everyone had left and pulled down their pants. The other boy's penis was hard and he helped Desmond, then became so excited he did it for the younger boy, climaxing himself when Desmond did.

That had been so many years ago. Father Desmond stroked the sleek, bountiful body of Calida. A year later he had found out about girls. A cousin of his on a picnic had teased him and ran into the woods. He followed and when he found her she had her blouse open and showed him her growing breasts. She had been fourteen and well developed.

She quickly opened his pants, and played with him, but before she could get her skirt and drawers off, he had ejaculated and she hit him in the eye and ran off just mad as hell.

After that he pumped off his pud, as he called it, twice a week. But it wasn't until he was fifteen that he actually had intercourse. She had been fifteen, too, that summer, as curious about boys as he was about girls.

They had piano lessons right after each other, and that Saturday afternoon walking home after the lessons, they stopped in a small park. She had kissed him first, "just for fun," she had told him. That led to more kisses and exploring and then a panting, passionate joining of their bodies both with all of their clothes still on.

She had been disappointed and never let him touch her again. He had been thrilled and started looking for "that kind of girl" who liked sex as much as he did.

Then he went to study for the priesthood and discovered that girls were not the only means for sexual relief. But he broke from that mold as soon as he could.

The first time he made love after he became an ordained priest, he was in abject misery for a week. At his confession that week he told his senior paster of his sin, and the older priest counseled him.

He said quite simply that before a priest is a priest, he must be a man. Man is a sexual being, he can't live normally without some sexual feelings. The senior priest told Desmond to be careful, to beat down those feelings whenever he could. If he occasionally fell from grace, his confessor, and

114

surely God himself who made man a sexual creature, would understand.

The bishop did not understand. Nor did the husband of one of the biggest givers to the church.

Father Desmond began a round of singularly unpopular, poor and hard to serve parishes.

Now he smiled as he watched Calida. So innocent. She must be kept that way. Innocent in all ways except sexually. She had gladly provided him with every type of sexual gratification he asked of her. But still a child.

She looked up and smiled. "Father, may I have the honor of undressing you?" she asked.

He nodded. One last time.

As she took off his priestly habit, he watched her, noted her every movement, every smile, each crease in her beautiful face when she smiled. Small wrinkles on her forehead as she frowned. Soft, dark eyes, thin, yet sensuous lips.

Mostly he watched the movement of her breasts as she undressed him. So perfect, so beautiful! Woman was breasts! So delicately formed, so useful, so marvelously picturesque! If he were a poet he would write a sonnet to breasts.

When she had stripped off all his clothes, he contrasted his starkly white skin with her golden brown. Her skin was beautiful. His pathetic. At five six he was not a big man, but he had stayed in passable shape. Sometimes this was because he ate nothing but whiskey for three days at a time.

He smiled. He had been slightly drunk in Houston. It had caused the bishop to vow his vengeance. The woman involved had known of Father Desmond's weakness. She had reason to work in the church office now and then, and had heard stories.

He was sure she had set out to trap him. She had a tantalizing way of showing up when he was alone, and then telling him how much she admired him. Six times she had seen him when they were alone, in the garden, the church library, once in the confessional. Each time she moved closer to showing him that she would not mind his advances.

But this time he had held true! He had resisted. The final blow came when he received a note from a messenger. The woman needed him at her home at once. An emergency! He hurried there thinking something had happened to her.

She let him in, looking worried. She wore a heavy robe and hurried ahead of him up the stairs and into the master bedroom. She had locked the door behind them, waved him forward into the bathroom, where a large tub had been specially built into the end of the room.

Calmly she dropped the robe and was naked.

"Father Desmond, I want you to take a bath with me, and any other interesting games we might figure out to play." She had smiled and kissed him, then undressed him and led him into the tub filled with warm water and bubbles.

He had fallen from Grace, deep and hard. The third time they left the water and used the big bed. That was when her husband walked into the bedroom. She had planned it all along. She didn't mind getting caught, as long as she could take him down. The bishop transferred him immediately.

Father Desmond caressed Calida's young body and then gently they made love. He had never felt more satisfaction, more at peace. How had he fallen so far that he could find peace when defying the church, breaking his vows?

He held her in his arms. She was one woman who

wanted nothing from him, who wanted only to give to him, perhaps in return for some love and tenderness. She was too good for him, but he refused to share her with anyone.

Slowly he eased her to the bed, sat up at his small desk and wrote a letter. He started it a second time, then had it the way he wanted it. He dated and signed it. Then he sealed it in an envelope, wrote a name on the outside and went back to the bed.

She must not know, he must keep her pure and clean and innocent before God. He sat beside her on the bed, stroked her, petted her marvelous young form.

"Calida, put your head in my lap and close your eyes," he told her gently. He bent and kissed her cheek. "I'll always love you, small one," he said softly.

Then with a knife he had brought with him from the desk, he slit her precious throat, slicing through the big artery on the side of her neck. For a moment she struggled. He held her. In ten seconds she was dead, her blood gushed out of her carotid artery, soaking his legs and the bed.

Swiftly he gave her the last rites. He was crying then, softly with many tears. He prayed again, purifying her soul, then clasped his bloody hands and asked for his own forgiveness.

He bent again and kissed her bloody cheek, then slit his own throat and fell on top of her in death as swift as hers.

12

McCoy was up and moving with the sun the next morning. He left Beth tangled in the sheet after kissing her cheek. He had a quick breakfast and then walked the streets. Everything was calm. He saw a few people, but nowhere were there any black faces.

The men he saw were grim and tight lipped.

Marshal Garth Ludlow was also out patrolling.

"Looks quiet," Ludlow said.

"So far. I booted the mayor and his coloreds out of town until things cool down. Don't know how long I can keep them out."

"Blood will flow in the street if they come back today," Ludlow said.

"Probably." Spur looked toward the store front that served as City Hall. "Got me a feeling things are going to come to a head here soon. Maybe today. Is this the last day to pay city taxes?"

"Yep, without a penalty."

"You've raised a posse before, Marshal Ludlow?"

"One or two."

"Don't forget how. I'm hoping we won't have the

need. Got me a gut feeling."

"You think White will make a run for it?"

"Don't the Baggers always do that?"

"True. We watch the son of a bitch!"

"We watch everybody."

They nodded and went their ways around the waking town.

After making the rounds for another hour, Spur walked up to the Catholic church. It was quiet. No early Mass yet. He remembered his meeting with the priest and checked his pocket watch. Not quite eight. He was supposed to be here at nine. What's an hour early?

He walked in through the gate in the six-foot church wall around the garden. He knew the way to the priest's quarters. The parsonage had been set to one side, with an outside door through the wall. Spur had come in the long way. He saw a sister walking into the church and nodded.

He knocked on the front door and waited. There was no response. After a moment he knocked again. When there was no answer the second time he tried the door. It was unlocked. He eased it open and stepped inside.

Maybe the priest was at Mass after all, or confession. He waited a moment in the coolness of the room. It was nicely furnished with heavily built furniture and had a fireplace at the far end.

"Father Desmond?" he called softly. No answer. He tried again. Unusual. The priest should be up and about by now. A tension gripped him and he knew something was wrong. It happened sometimes.

Quickly he began to search the parsonage. At the end of the hall he found a locked door. Gently he tested the lock, then used the point of his pocket

knife between the door and casing and forced the
bolt back until the door unlocked and swung open.

It was a bedroom and at once he saw the huddled
bodies on the bed. Dried blood had made a deep red
stain over part of the sheet and on the naked bodies.
More blood had splashed and splattered on the floor.

He touched the priest's arm. It was cold, stiff.
Both had been dead for ten hours or more. He
wanted someone else to find the bodies. Spur wasn't
sure why. He looked around the room, saw the
envelope on a small desk and to his surprise it had
his name on it. Suicide note? He picked it up, folded
it and pushed it in his pocket, then hurried to the
bedroom door and stepped into the hall.

He made sure the door was set to lock behind him,
then closed it and went to the far door. He was right.
It opened on the street. When no one was looking, he
stepped through the door and into the street. He
walked rapidly away and back to Main Street.

He had seen death before, but never a priest and a
young girl in such an obviously wicked and sinful
situation. Murder and suicide, it had to be. He
leaned against the wall of a store and took out the
envelope.

It was sealed. Inside he found a piece of white
paper with the priest's name printed in the upper
left hand corner.

The writing was clear, bold and easy to read. A
practiced hand.

"My Dear Agent McCoy:
  "I take pen in hand this evening to confess
to you and to Almighty God my thousands of
sins and transgressions. I am not worthy to be
a priest, a vessel of God.
    "I have violated this marvelous child

called Calida. I have carnal knowledge of her, and have sinned repeatedly—yet she is my joy and my sanity in an insane world. Calida is as pure as new snow, as innocent as a newborn babe.

"I am a victim of my own excesses. I have loved John Barleycorn more than God. I have adored the gentle hand, the womanly caresses and ministrations of Calida more than I have loved and served Jesus Christ our Lord.

"Some years ago I was also involved in the deaths of twelve men. I have never confessed this sin to any priest, and now I do so to you hoping for absolution. It was a mistake that began as a lark, as a patriotic duty, and wound up in a furious battle that was to stain and cripple my priesthood ever after.

"Ever since it happened, I have regretted that act, and another recently when I was a factor in the untimely death of Harry Johnson. I am eternally damned, and eternally sorry for this monstrous and most grievous sin, for which I plead for forgiveness so I might dwell in the house of the Lord forever and ever.

"Now soon it will be over. I can't go on living with so much sin and violence and seductions and my repeated violations and corruption of this wonderful girl child, Calida.

"The time is here. It will be quick for her. She will not suffer. She will not even know what is to happen. She is soft and pure, an innocent in the eyes of God. May she live in heaven forever.

"Tell my new friends goodbye for me. Tell them that I lived as I wanted to, and now I die as I wish. Farewell. s/Father Ambrose Desmond."

* * *

Spur read the note again, looking for any nuances he had missed. Two items sparked his interest.

"Some years ago," the priest said he had been involved in the death of twelve men. How many years ago? Where? Here in Johnson Creek? Spur had no way of knowing. If only he could have asked the priest some questions.

He had the chance last night and turned the man away. By now Harry Johnson's death might have been cleared up. The priest said he was somehow involved in Harry's death.

"Damnit!" Spur said out loud.

A passing woman looked at him in shocked surprise and walked quickly away.

Spur snorted and refolded the letter and put it in his pocket. He was right in slipping away from the death scene. He wanted someone else to find them. There was a chance whoever was second in command at the church might want to make some changes before the law was called in.

The priest would account for the fifth gun that killed Harry Johnson, if all of Spur's theories and suspicious held together. Father Desmond was clearly despondent over his inability to live up to his priestly duties and code of conduct. Evidently he at last had taken his vows seriously and could not live knowing what he had done, how he had sinned.

If only Spur had talked to him last night!

He turned and walked down the street past the saddle shop. For a moment he wanted to go in and talk with the midget. He changed his mind. He would see June first. Priests had been known to use fancy ladies before, to keep everything simple and secret.

At June's shop the blinds were drawn with a note

pinned to them: "In fitting session. Closed for now. Please call again."

Spur spun around and went to see Beth at the bank. She was in. She closed the door to her new office and he saw that the two hunting prize mounted heads had been taken down from the wall and that a beautiful oil painting of an ocean scene now served as decoration in their place.

He eased into a chair across from her big desk that now was perfectly clean on top except for a pad of paper and a pencil. He watched the small, pretty girl with the deep brown eyes and smiled.

"Beth, that was quite a meeting we had last night," he said.

She smiled, her whole face seemed to glow, her large brown eyes sparkled with enthusiasm and for a moment a hot flash of desire boiled there.

"The most wonderful night of my life! How else can I describe it. Just marvelous. Tonight I want you at my house for dinner and then we can . . . talk after dinner."

"We'll see. Things are happening. I might have found the fifth man in the five gun mystery. What I want to ask now is for you to think again about any groups your father might have been in that had five other men, or more."

"Groups, groups." She stood and walked around the office, came up behind him and kissed his cheek, then moved away, her face serious, concentrating.

"For about five years he was on the Board of Trustees at church. There were six or seven of them. Yes, he was on the school board for a four year term, but that was five or six years ago. What else?"

Spur turned to look at her staring out her window at Main Street. "None of those groups seems quite like the type of men we're hunting. Although I suppose they might be. If we don't know who we're looking for, it could be anybody. That's McCoy's law.''

"Last time I mentioned the poker club he was in for the past four or five years. Then I think he went riding with a friend or two for a while, a kind of trail club, where they went on rides through the country just for fun. The cowboys thought they were crazy."

"Riding club. Who was in it?"

"Not sure. I didn't pay any attention. Oh, wait, yes Walt Trembolt the blacksmith was one of them."

"I've met Mr. Trembolt. He seems like a man who gets excited quickly. That may be a start."

She paced again. "There was a group at church called the Sociables. They met once a month for outings, picnics, pot luck suppers, church kind of socials. Mostly couples in it from young to middle aged."

"Not likely our people. The poker club. Do you remember anyone who was involved in it."

"He never talked about that one. Maybe once or twice." She turned and stared at him, her eyes wide, surprise and worry tingeing her features.

"Yes! I remember one name. He remarked two or three times what a good cherry pie that Mrs. Runner always served every time they had the game at the Runner's home!"

"Hans Runner, one of the men we think might be in on the cover-up of your father's death." Spur stood up quickly. "Let me talk to some other people. Some of the card players might know about such a game, especially if it was a regular thing and had a closed group who played. Most real gamblers dream about getting in a continuing game like that."

Spur reached into an inside shirt pocket and took

out a much folded letter that had traveled from Johnson Creek to Washington D.C. and now he had brought it back where it began.

"We're making progress, Beth. Now, I want to show you the letter your father wrote to us. Read it and see if you can help us fill in any of the empty spots."

He handed her the letter and she read:

"Gentlemen. My name is Harry Johnson from Johnson Creek, Texas. I need your help. Some years ago I was involved in an act that I considered at the time to be legal and patriotic, but which it turned out was neither.

"Now I want to clear my conscience and return to the Federal Government something it has lost. I have no trust in our current Carpetbagger local government, and little more trust in the county or state governments.

"I wish to deal directly with a respresent-ative of some U.S. law enforcement agency, such as a U.S. Marshal. I am sure that you will not be disappointed if you send someone to talk to me. This would have to be categorized as a confession, and as such I am ready to stand trial and accept any punishment that the court feels justified to levy.

"I hope this can be taken care of quickly, since I am not the only person involved in this situation. Your every consideration to my request will be greatly appreciated. Yours truly, Harry Johnson, President of the Johnson Bank of Johnson Creek, Texas."

Beth lowered the paper. Tears seeped from her eyes. She made no move to dry them. Her voice was so soft he could hardly hear her when she spoke.

"I can't believe it. But I know that is Daddy's writing. He must have been roped into something not knowing what it was. Or maybe they made him help them. Whoever they are. Maybe Hans Runner and the others forced him to ride with them."

Spur put his arms around her and she cried on his chest for a moment, then leaned back.

"I'd . . . I'd like to keep this letter."

"Of course. What I'm thinking now, is that the other five found out about this letter. Maybe your father even told them. They decided they couldn't let him confess and involve the rest of them."

"Damn them all!" Beth said savagely. Her tone surprised Spur.

"Beth, I don't want you looking for vengeance. Leave this to me. I'll find the men who shot your father and they will be punished. Promise me you won't go wild and do something that will get both of us in trouble."

He still held her. She looked up and now wiped the tears away. She nodded.

Gently she pushed away from him and went back to her desk. She sat down, wiped her eyes with a small white handkerchief, then looked up at him.

"Oh, Don White came in today. He said he needed twenty-five hundred dollars to pay county bills. He explained to me that the council has set a new policy of cash payments."

"I hope you didn't give any money to him."

"No, I stalled as you directed me to. I told him it would take me two or three days to get that much cash money for him. He went crazy mad, threatened to start a run on the bank and ruin me. He swore that he had to have the cash by today at closing time, or at least by five o'clock.

"Don't give him a dime. He's getting ready to run, so he needs cash. Has he made any deposits of the tax money? He must be taking in thousands at the city office."

"He made one deposit three days ago, but none since then." She paused. "Is he really getting ready to abscond with our money?"

"Looks like it. But that's my problem. Today is the last day to pay taxes. He'll be gone tonight . . . if he can."

He stood and went around the desk.

"Sorry I had to show you that letter, but I wanted the air to be clear, and everything straight between us. No secrets. Now, I need to talk to June again." He grinned. "You sure were right about her figure. I don't think I've ever seen such big . . ."

Beth's hand went quickly over his mouth.

"Sir. It's not polite to praise another woman about her big cow breasts when you're standing toe to toe with the smallest tits in town." Beth laughed, her good humor had returned. "You just be sure to keep your hands off her. I'll take care of any of your wild sexy needs tonight."

He kissed her lips gently, and hurried out the door. Beth Johnson was quite a little bundle of woman.

June was in and free. He sat in a chair near her cutting table and watched her work on a flat piece of cloth. She gave him a cold bottle of Zang's beer.

"June, I'm making progress, but I need some more help."

"In back with our clothes off, or out here?" she said with a quick grin.

"Unfortunately, out here. Do you remember something strange and illegal happening three or four years ago? Something that was hushed up or not even known to most of the people in town? It probably involved Harry Johnson and some of the biggest men in the community."

She cut on the cloth, concentrating for a few moments. When she finished she looked up and lifted her brows.

"I guess confidences aren't important to Harry anymore. Yeah, there was something. His wife has been dead for some time, and maybe once or twice a year he'd send me a note and come over late at night. This time he was a little drunk and he drank more after he arrived and as I remember, he couldn't even get his pants off.

"He wanted to talk, mostly. So we talked for two hours and then he paid me ten dollars. He said once years before he got drunk with some other men and they started bragging and the first thing he knew they were armed and riding north. He and the others shot up some men in a camp.

"He never said much more about who they were or what happened, but evidently the men in the woods all died. He said they all thought it was going to be one harassing attack against the enemy. Now I remember. He said it was to be one last angry strike at the Yankees, even though they knew the South had almost lost the war."

Spur nodded. "So, just near the end of the war. Some raid. Maybe he was one of a defense force here in town, something like that. I'll do some research. Harry ever mention this again?"

"He never came back. Maybe he wasn't quite as drunk as he pretended to be and just had to tell somebody. The way Catholics go to confession."

Spur agreed. "Thanks, June. You've been a big help."

She grinned. "Spur McCoy, for you my door is always open. And by that I mean my bedroom door. Anytime."

Spur smiled, touched her shoulder and hurried out to the boardwalk, eager to make his next call.

13

Spur saw the midget working away on a saddle, his
back to the door. McCoy eased inside, closed the
door silently, sat in the chair and laid his feet gently
on the edge of a small, cold stove.

Without turning around, the small man, Big Paul
Smith, spoke. "Not bad for a Secret Agent. But you
got to remember that your left boot squeaks when
you walk and you drop your right shoulder just a
tad like you're getting ready to draw."

He turned around and grinned. "Hi, McCoy. I still
say that Sir Frances Bacon was the most brilliant
man of his day."

Spur laughed. "How in hell did you know it was
me? Nobody is that good. Heard someone, maybe,
but how did you know?"

"Look over there by that rolled leather. What do
you see?"

Spur looked where the small man pointed. A four-
inch square mirror had been fixed to the leather bin.
When Spur looked in it he saw Big Paul Smith grin-
ning at him.

"You cheated," Spur said.

"Another one over there," Smith said waving at the other side of his shop. I got you covered two ways."

"No contest," Spur said. He lifted his hat and let it settle down over his eyes. "Get back to work, Paul, you can't make any money mouth-jawing with an out of work drifter."

"So true you are, Secret Agent McCoy. How goes the investigation?" Smith slid back onto his stool and went to work on the saddle.

"It's slow. These Carpetbaggers don't help any. What I need is some history. How long you been playing with leather around this town?"

"Little over ten years, man and boy."

"All man. Do you remember when the war was almost over, say about four years ago?"

"Yep. Remember it like it was yesterday. We had a few raids by irregulars. Might have been Northerners, or Southerners, we never knew. A month before the surrender a batch went through one night. Killed two men, raped three or four women, we were never sure, and took a wagon load of food out of the general store."

"Things were a bit touchy here then I'd guess."

"True as blue. We had sort of a home guard. Couple of dozen of the older men who couldn't go to war, and a few of the younger ones who went and came back. Young Garth Ludlow headed the outfit. He was a wounded veteran, and after the last raid they had regular meetings, practiced with their rifles, the whole thing. As I remember they called themselves the Mounted Home Guard."

"You knew the war was going badly for the South?"

"Hell yes. Everybody knew. We was just sort of sitting here wondering after it was over what would happen and when it was going to happen. We expected northern troops to be all over the place as an occupation force."

"How did the men take the coming loss?"

"Damn mad, most of them. Ones who didn't go to war wished to hell they had. Them that were sent home, wished they had stayed on and helped. Frustrated, the whole town was mad as hell and frustrated.

"One day I heard about an offensive raid the Home Guard was going to make. Kind of a last hurrah, one more sting at the hated Bluebellies. Never did hear what happened. Come to think of it, Garth was talking it up like crazy one day, and it seemed like they were going out that night or the next."

The small man put down a leather tool and scratched his nose. "Damn, after that I don't remember Garth saying a word about it. Don't know if they even went or not. Then we heard the war was over. Guess it was all settled a week or two before we knew about it."

Big Paul Smith scratched his thinning brown hair. "Damn, come to think of it, don't remember anybody mentioning that proposed 'raid' again."

"Who were in the Home Guard, you remember any of them?"

"It broke up, of course when the war was over. But I sure as the English Bard himself can't think of any others. One, yeah, I remember one more. Harry Johnson was in it. Told me once he signed up just so he could get in on the riding. Harry did love to fork a horse. He was planning on buying himself a little spread and raise a few beef. He never got around to it."

"It's too late for him to be starting now," Spur

said dropping his feet off the stove. He sat up. "Any more names in that Home Guard you can remember?"

"Jess Holloway. But he moved to California a year or so back. They had twelve or fifteen for one parade, but it went up and down. One night I saw them drilling with only four men."

Spur stood, watched the small man working on the tooling of the leather for a minute. "I'm glad you're not an engraver and that isn't a plate for a twenty dollar bill."

"Tried that once, but I kept putting my own picture on the fifty dollar bill!"

"Should have worked. Thanks for the history lesson. Never know what's going to fit in."

"Welcome. And the next time you need a good saddle . . ."

"I'll stop back."

Spur walked into the morning sunlight. He had most of the pieces. But why would a Home Guard charge into a twelve man patrol of some sort? And was it U.S. Army, or some irregulars, or some border bandits that roamed the line between the North and the South in those terrible days?

He walked part way down the block when he saw Marshal Ludlow striding quickly toward him. Garth looked up and motioned.

"Better come with me, McCoy. We have new trouble. Seems like somebody has killed the priest, Father Desmond."

A few minutes later the two lawmen looked over the priest's bedroom. The large red stain still showed on the rumpled sheets and dried blood coated part of the floor below his figure. Father Desmond lay crumpled on the side of the bed where he had been before. He wore a simple white nightgown.

The young naked girl Spur had seen lying in his lap had been taken away.

Marshal Ludlow bent and looked at the body, tried to move an arm.

"Damn! He's stiff already. Been dead for hours. Why in hell would someone want to murder a priest in his bed?"

A nun came forward. She wore a long black robe and white collar and headpiece that covered all her hair and allowed only a circle of face to show.

"Marshal, I'm Mother Superior Mary Angeles. I found him this way. It looks like someone robbed him. We found the side door open. The lock had been forced from the outside. We suggest that someone broke in, waited for Father Desmond to return, assaulted him sometime last night, and then the intruder took his time lookng for valuables."

Marshal Ludlow nodded. "Seems reasonable. Is anything missing?"

"Oh, yes. We had over twenty dollars in the Altar Fund, and about fifty dollars from our poor box collections. Father Desmond liked to keep the money on hand so he could spend it as we needed to. A gold crucifix is missing as well as three rings Father treasured. One had been blessed by the Pope."

Ludlow made some quick notes on a pad of paper he had brought.

"Any value on the rings, Mother Superior?"

"Sentimental value on one. Father Desmond told me the others were given to him by his parents when he was ordained. Both were worth over a hundred dollars."

"So we can say the robber took the valuables and cash worth three hundred and seventy dollars."

"Begging your pardon, Marshal," Mother

Superior Angeles said. "The killer also took something much more valuable. A loyal servant of God. He took the life of Father Desmond."

"Was anyone else hurt?" Spur asked gently.

Mother Superior's head lifted and she looked quickly at Spur. Too quickly.

"No. No one. We didn't know he was . . . was dead until his housekeeper came in this morning. He usually doesn't sleep in mornings. But she decided he was taking a nap since his inside bedroom door was locked. An hour later she went around and found the street door open. She hurried and told me and I went in and found him. I didn't want the others to see this."

"We understand, Mother Superior," Spur said. "I think we have enough here, don't you, Marshal?"

Ludlow stared at the bloody, waxy figure on the bed and nodded. "Enough to last me for some time."

Outside Marshal Ludlow took off his high crowned brown hat and scratched his hair. "Don't rightly know, McCoy. But to me it looked like too damn much blood around there for just one body to lose. Especially when his throat was slit. Man dies in just a few seconds when that side artery is cut. When the heart stops pumping, the blood stops gushing out. Too damn much blood back there."

"Maybe a priest bleeds more than other men," Spur said.

"Maybe." They walked in silence for a while. "Now that Mother Superior. She was hard as a hickory fence post. She never batted an eyebrow. Tough, efficient. Looks like the kind of person who can get things done."

"Yep, I agree. She can get things done. You figure it was one of the blacks who cut the priest?"

"One of the coloreds? Could have been. One of

them could have been eyeing that priest, slipped back into town last night after dark, slit him and took the loot."

"Possible." Spur looked over at the shorter man. "I hear you used to have a Mounted Home Guard in town during the war. Was Harry Johnson in it?"

"Don't rightly know. I remember hearing about it."

"You did that. In fact you started it after you got back from fighting in the gray uniform. Was Harry in it, too?"

Marshal Ludlow stopped and scratched his chin. "Yeah, I think so, toward the last. It was a tough time. We got raided three or four times by Yankee irregulars. Lost three men the last time, so we decided to put up a fight after that."

"Did you?"

"Hell no. Never got raided again and then the war was over, and we forgot all about the Home Guard. Had enough new problems with Reconstruction and the damn Baggers."

"Life does get complicated."

"You heard from Don White today?" Garth asked. "What in hell is he planning on doing? You know?"

"Probably planning on leaving town. But he won't go without all the money he can steal. That's your job. Watch City Hall and hire a deputy to watch that grove of trees two miles south along that little creek. That's where I took White and his in-the-pocket voters yesterday."

"I'll keep him covered."

"Keep him away from the bank. There's three thousand worth of city money in there he wants."

"I'll let him go in, but I'll be right behind him. He must be ready to run."

"Today is the last day to pay city taxes. This is the most money the city will have in its till all year. Tonight has to be his time, or perhaps tomorrow. The bank is the key. He needs the cash in there."

"Don't worry, it's covered."

Spur watched Ludlow. "I'm still interested in this Home Guard. You must remember some of the other men who were in it. I'd like to talk to some of them. I'm a student of the Civil War. It was a classic struggle, but I've never understood the border states position very well."

"Some of them died, three or four moved on. Harry was in it, I remember now, and Walt the blacksmith. I don't think the hardware man was in . . . but then he left town anyway. Went busted I hear."

"Did you have any medical men? Doc Greenly. Was he in town then?"

"Think he moved here after the war. It all gets kind of fuzzy back there, trying to remember."

"You remember, Ludlow. I want a list of every man you can think of who was in the Home Guard. I'll pick it up tomorrow."

Ludlow looked at up Spur and for a moment hatred flared there, then it faded. The town marshal nodded and walked off toward the bank.

14

Don White woke up that morning feeling gritty, with a bad taste in his mouth and a screaming headache. One more goddamn day! He had to get it done today and be gone with the darkness. It had worked before in Georgia, it would work here.

He was in the house he had rented with city money at the edge of town. Despite the Secret Agent's warning, he had sneaked back into the house from the grove as soon as it was dark. He had to run the city office for one more day. Yesterday he had hired a white woman to accept tax payments.

He made sure he found an honest one, a Baptist, a good churchgoer, Mrs. Hemphil. There was no worry there. He just had to be sure he got there before she tried to deposit the money in the bank. He had no idea what was wrong at the bank. Just his luck to run into some kind of an internal bank problem.

He sat up in his short underwear and wished he had a bath. He couldn't risk starting a fire to heat water. He called in one of the blacks.

"Willy, bring me a bucket of water from that

pump out in the woodshed. Be sure nobody sees you
or hears you, or you could be one dead darkie. You
understand?''

The big colored man nodded and hurried out for a
bucket.

White took a whore's bath in the bucket of cold
water and thought over his haul. He had two
thousand in cash in a valise hidden in the cupboard.
There was over a thousand in checks for taxes some
of the merchants had written for him before he made
it a rule of cash only.

He had to get to the bank and cash those. There
could be no problem there. He would go in just
before the bank closed at three. There would be
plenty of time after that.

Then there was more than two thousand in the
city account deposited in the bank. He had to figure
out a way to withdraw that without attracting any
suspicion.

He stretched out on the bed in his shirt and clean
white pants. "Damn, but this is going to be a good
one!" he said softly, then chuckled.

So they told him in Chicago he would never
amount to anything. What the hell did they know?
He was soon to be a rich man with over five
thousand dollars, cash money, in his poke!

Not a one of those fancy Dans in Chicago would
have a fifth that much, right now.

It just took some brains, a little bit of luck, and
the guts to put it to the damn Southerners.

Ruth came in wearing that little red French
nightie he bought for her in Houston. It barely
covered her crotch and left both her breasts
swinging and bouncing free. On her it looked great.

She dropped down beside him on the bed and
leaned over him letting her breasts swing out above

him like a pair of upside down ice cream cones.

"Kiss my ladies good morning, handsome prince," she said. He did, licking the nipples, but then pushing her away.

"Get your pussy out of here, Ruth. Right now I got some thinking to do. Today has got to go just right."

"We getting ready to run out on the bastards?"

"We're not running out, we're starting our advance on Houston. Whoever gets left behind, gets left. My buggy will only carry three."

"Hey, I'm glad that I'm one of the three."

He smiled at her and went back to planning. First the bank, get the money on deposit if he had to rob the damn bank, then move out in the buggy to the grove south of town and trade the buggy for the fastest horses he could find. They were saddled, fed and watered and would be ready to go at six o'clock.

There would be room enough for the money in his saddlebags. No one else was going to have a look at the cash. He called to Ruth and stroked her sleek young breasts. She said she was seventeen but he didn't believe her.

She had been the best thing about this little episode. What a delightful young body, and such good tits! Yes, she was a sex machine that never got tired and never was out of the mood. He'd found her in a fancy woman house in New Orleans and rescued her from twenty tricks a day. She was grateful. And she was getting to be a bore.

He pushed her away again. Another state, another bunch of suckers and another woman. Would he go back to Chicago? Not yet. Not when he could make five thousand in six or seven months. It could take a year depending on the next election time. He'd move until he found the right spot—preferably one that had not been swindled by another Carpetbagger from up north.

Christ but these assholes were stupid. Didn't they know what he was going to do? It had been in all the big papers. The farther out in the sticks the better. They *trusted* their elected officials.

He had come south on a whim, a fluke almost. He'd been drinking with this tall queer guy who was buying him drinks and trying to get him to come up to his apartment and play pull a prick with him.

White knew his capacity for beer. He figured he'd take the asshole for six beers, then push him off his stool and walk out of the bar. The queer said he had just come back from Mississippi where he had played Carpetbagger. White had urged him to talk about it.

For two hours the queer had told him exactly how to do it. How to scoop up enough coloreds and promise to pay them, and get them to vote you into office, mayor preferably, or supervisor or director, whatever the county administrator was called. He said he had stripped the treasury of this little county of almost ten thousand dollars.

White had gone willingly when the asshole invited him up to his flat to look at the newspaper clippings about him being elected director of the county.

By that time the queer had White's pants off and was playing around with him. It took him another ten minutes before White had all the information he could glean from the tall queer. Then White punched him out, tied him up and put his own pants back on. He tore the place apart until he found a stash of money, over a thousand dollars in cash!

White set the queer on his own window ledge and told him to tell him where the rest of the money was. He nodded that he would, but when White took the gag out, he screamed. White pushed him out of the fifth floor window and he bellowed all the way to the concrete below.

That same night, White left for the south and had been there ever since. Two years now.

And now another pay day.

Ruth had dressed and watched him.

"I wanna go to the store and buy some perfume," she said. Her voice was starting to irritate him.

"You go downtown and some white hothead will blow your guts out with a shotgun. Ain't you got any sense?"

"Still wanna buy some perfume and a new dress."

"We'll get both for you in Houston. Now sit down and shut up your big mouth, woman!"

For a moment she flared in anger, then she remembered how he had beat her the first week, and the anger turned to a smile.

"You always tell me my cunt is bigger than my mouth." She walked toward him unbuttoning her thin blouse. "Maybe my man would like a nice fast mouth job about now. Just go on doing whatever you're doing, don't mind me. All you have to do is sit up. I'll do the rest."

He had been thinking about tonight and leafing through a magazine. White grinned, shook his head and sat up. At once she was in front of him kneeling on the bedroom floor. She spread his legs and opened his pants fly and pulled them down.

She gave a little cry when she saw that he was stiff already.

"Now just relax, sir. This won't hurt a bit. It shouldn't take too long. Try to relax and let yourself go."

She slid his erection into her mouth, her hands busy with his scrotum.

"Easy on my balls! Oh, damn, where did you learn to eat cock so good!" She pointed at him and he laughed as she sucked his whole prick into her mouth and began bouncing up and down.

He couldn't concentrate on the magazine. At last he swore softly and tossed the reading matter aside. His hips began to counter her forward motion and she gagged once, then adapted and after ten more strokes he started to sweat.

"Christ but you are good with the mouth, Ruthie! Never seen a whore or any cunt who was as good with the mouth as you are. You bite me and I'll tear your tits off!"

She laughed and she sucked and it was more than he could stand. He humped straight up and she sagged, then swallowed and moved slightly but stayed with him until he shot his last load and collapsed on the bed.

She snaked up beside him, kissing his man breasts and tweaking his small nipples.

"Now, Big Daddy, wasn't that worth the price of the ticket?"

He grabbed both her breasts and squeezed.

"Nice, nice!" she wailed.

"Hey, don't get started again. I can't be worn out for the big push this afternoon."

"Whatever you say. I always do exactly what you tell me to do. That's why we make such a good team. You and me, babe."

"Yeah, yeah. You and me. Now I've got to go downtown and get the rest of the cash. You pack that little bag of yours and be ready to travel light. I'll be back here about five this afternoon with the buggy."

She leaned over top of him where he still lay on his back. He hadn't even buttoned up his fly. A sharp pointed knife caressed his throat.

"Tell me again, Big Daddy, that you're taking me with you to Houston. Taking me all the way. I don't care what you tell them blacks out there. It's you and me, right?"

"I told you, damnit. Move that blade."

"Tell me again, Babe. I want to hear you say it again."

"Ruthie, baby, you know I couldn't get along without them big tits of yours and that sweet, dancing pussy. Damn right you go with me. So pack and be ready."

She nicked his throat with the blade, then reached up and kissed it.

"Just a reminder, sweetheart. Nobody runs out on Ruthie. One man tried it. I killed him. Had to go across three states but I found him and put this same knife dead center into his black heart. So I'm glad to hear it's just you and me."

She leaped off the bed and held the knife in front of her. White had never seen it before.

"You got to learn to trust people, Ruthie. I said you was going, so you're going. Now get packed."

He buttoned his fly and walked out of the room. On the other side of the door he stopped and a deadly fury filled his face. He started to go back in, then shook his head and went on to the small back porch and woodshed. From there he could get into the alley.

He needed to check City Hall, see how the money was coming in, and collect it two or three times, so the new white lady clerk did not become upset about having all that cash around.

As he stood in the woodshed one of the men came up to him. He was Fred Washington. The Washington was new, the Fred was also new with his new freedom. He was a hulking field hand, who would never learn to do anything else.

Among the colored voters, White had named him as the enforcer. If anyone got out of line, they had to answer to Fred. Few went against the rules more than once.

In Houston Fred had a few too many beers one night, and nearly tore an arm off a longshoreman on the docks. Two of his buddies stormed up to help and he shattered one's arm and broke the second man's neck.

Fred got away just before the police came, but nobody who saw it had the nerve to turn in Fred for the killing.

Now he watched Don White.

"You say we're going soon," Fred asked.

"Don't worry about it. I said I was going to go to City Hall. Don't try to start thinking at this point, Fred. Just keep Ruth in the house and all three of you stay out of sight. Where is Willy?"

"Sleeping. He saw Ruthie all naked and he jerked off in his hand again."

"Let him sleep. Don't worry about a thing, Fred. Haven't I been taking care of you, and paying you?"

Fred nodded.

"Sure I have. And I always will, Fred. You'll never have to worry about trying to find a job again."

Fred nodded and went back in the house. White let out a long pent up breath and wiped some sweat off his forehead with the back of his hand. That big ape could break him in half with his bare hands. In twelve hours he'd be rid of them, all of them. He snorted. Even Fred, and Ruthie. Especially Ruthie.

Five minutes later, Fred slipped into the alley that led to the City Hall back doors. He found one unlocked as it was always supposed to be, and went inside. This was the back of an old feed store, and still smelled like alfalfa hay, oats and cracked corn.

He went through the door into the finished front section and looked out a second door at Mrs. Hemphil who sat behind the desk marked "Pay City Taxes Here."

Two people stood in line.

White walked out casually, approached Mrs. Hemphil when she had finished with one of those waiting.

"How are we doing this morning, Mrs. Hemphil?"

She was flustered for a moment, then she recovered. "Oh, well, yes. Things are going smoothly. Some people complain because the taxes went up, but I tell them I didn't do it, they should talk to their city council."

"Absolutely correct, Mrs. Hemphil. Let me take your cash box out for deposit. We don't want to tempt anyone here, do we?"

She smiled and slid the cash drawer to him. He carried it quickly to the back room, emptied out the drawer of all but a few ones and two fives and a ten and put the bills into his pocket. There must be three or four hundred!

He took the cash drawer back to Mrs. Hemphil, told her what a good job she was doing, and went to his small office. Inside he opened a cabinet and looked at a sheaf of checks. A paper clip on top of them pinned a paper to the checks. It had a figure, One thousand, three hundred and seventy-two dollars.

That presented a problem. The bankers seemed all upset and nervous about something. Even Beth Johnson was acting funny. He decided to try to cash the checks around noon, when there were more people in the bank. They might want to rush him through so a line wouldn't form.

Yes, he would try that. He put the checks in an envelope. Each check had been endorsed by the city in the person of Mrs. Hemphil, acting city clerk. They were ready for cashing. He put the envelope in his inside jacket pocket.

What was the girl's name in Chicago? He could hardly remember. He would never go back there, he was certain now. With five thousand dollars he could afford to buy more voters, hit a bigger town or county where he would need to produce maybe two hundred votes to swing an election.

Now he'd have the money to finance it. Give each of the blacks a dollar to sign on with him and two dollars a week. Or get some Human Welfare program started to let the county or city pay them.

What was the girl's name in Chicago? She wasn't built half as well as Ruthie. She probably had never been touched. Ruthie could fuck rings around that girl.

He put his hands behind his head and leaned back in the chair. Yes, Houston for a few weeks, living it up, eating the best food he could find. Maybe a quick trip over to New Orleans for some tremendous food and entertainment.

Yeah! He'd heard if you have enough money in New Orleans you can buy a woman who will do anything. He even heard you could absolutely fuck yourself to death over there. Now that would be a damn nice way to go. If you wanted to go. Don White wasn't ready yet for any kind of thinking. But he did have a hankering to be in New Orleans when he could afford to sample any of its pleasures that he wanted.

He grinned, then put his business face on and got up and headed for the Johnson Bank.

15

As he walked, Spur McCoy watched the townspeople. They were still jittery, on edge, half expecting the fifty Negroes to charge into town with guns blazing, looting and raping. They had every right to be afraid. Worse things had happened by the newly freed Negroes in some parts of the South after the war.

But this was Texas. There was a sputtering of vigilante movement, but from what Spur could guess, no real leader to take over and organize it. That was one big problem he didn't have to worry about.

When he got to the bank it was nearly noon. Inside, he went to Beth's private office and walked through the open door. She wore a patterned brown dress with a little jacket and looked almost businesslike. Spur could not get used to this twig of a girl sitting behind the president's desk of the town's bank.

"Good morning, I'd like to borrow a hundred thousand dollars," Spur said before she looked up.

She laughed and went on writing on a paper.

"Fine, leave your wife and first born as collateral, and I'll draw up the papers at once," she said. Beth looked up and a wonderful smiled transformed her face.

"I'm glad to see you." Then she frowned. "The new city clerk tried to cash six checks this morning. I turned her down, saying there had been a hold put on that account by the Federal Government." She stood and watched Spur closely. "Was that all right? I didn't know what else to say. I'm afraid Don White will storm over here shouting and screaming."

"If he does call me and I'll throw him out."

"You might be busy."

"Let's shelve that problem for a while. I'll take you out for a bite of dinner."

"Oh good!" She looked down and blushed softly. "My . . . my feet still haven't quite come to the ground yet . . . after last night. That was the most wonderful . . ."

One of the tellers came in with some papers. She looked at them, signed the bottom of one and he left.

Spur grinned. "It was wonderful for me too. Now, some food. Then we can worry about White."

At the Demorest Family restaurant they had big bowls of vegetable soup and slabs of fresh baked bread and home made jam. As they ate, Spur told her what he had found out about her father.

"So the jist of it seems to be that your father was a member of the Mounted Guard back near the end of the war. Something happened back there that evidently involved these six men. Now somehow that old event has caused some problems, including your father's death. I'm still digging into it."

Beth sat still for a moment, then nodded. "Yes, I remember the Mounted Home Guards. Daddy was so pleased that he joined. He loved to ride his horse Prince, a big gelding that could outrun anything in town." A tear ran down her cheek.

"I . . . I still miss him so. I guess I'm an orphan now, right?"

"Absolutely, and the only orphan I know of who owns her own bank and about half of the town."

"Oh, that. I'd rather have Daddy back."

"I'd evict three widows and their kids if it would bring him back, Beth. So we do the next best thing. You run the bank the same thoughtful, friendly way your father did. And I'll find out who killed him."

They finished the soup and each had another half a slice of the still warm bread.

"Isn't it terrible about Father Desmond? I don't understand how anybody could kill a priest."

Spur nodded, wondering if he should tell her. He decided against it. When he knew everything about the Home Guard and what happened so long ago, he might tell her. Not now.

"Well, I couldn't eat another bite," Spur said. "Let's go back to the bank and wait for Don White. He's probably mad enough by now to come storming in."

As soon as they walked into the bank, Don White marched up to them.

"What's this about a Federal order to put a hold on the city's bank account?" he asked, his voice only barely pleasant with an undercurrent of fury. "You know the town can't operate without funds from its account."

"Mr. White. You've caused a lot of problems in this town. Some fine people have been hurt badly, and all because of you. From now on I'm doing everything I can to drive you out of office. It's my bank. Legally I can freeze your account if I want to.

Try and find a law that says I can't.

"Now, if you have any problems with that, you go find a good lawyer and sue me. The circuit judge will be around in about two months, I'll talk to you in court then."

He stared at her, his anger rising by the second. He tightened both hands into fists, then looked at Spur who stood directly behind Beth staring hard at White.

He tried to talk, but his anger had forced his voice into a rumble. He shook his head, tried to relax his hands, then at last got the words out.

"I want to close out the city account. Everything in cash right now."

"No. That account has been frozen pending an investigation by Federal authorities. Please leave my bank, now, Mr. White, or you will be forcibly ejected."

White's face turned red. His eyelids lifted showing the whites of his eyes and Spur thought he might have a stroke. He trembled, his hands fisted again but he never stepped toward Beth. Slowly he turned and walked woodenly toward the door. As he opened the heavy door, he looked back, and Spur could not remember seeing a face showing more hatred. Then he was gone.

Beth leaned back against Spur and gave a big sigh.

"I've never been so frightened!" she whispered to him.

"You were great, Beth. You stopped him in his tracks and sent him running." Spur scowled for a moment. "How much money in the city account?"

"I checked this morning. A little over two thousand dollars."

"By now he thinks it's his money. He swindled it

fair and square. The next time he comes back to the bank it'll be with guns. Do you have a bank guard?"

"No, we've never needed one."

"You do now. See if you can hire a man with a good shotgun for the job. Do it quietly. Get him on the job in half an hour or so. Do you have any idea who you can get?"

"Yes. An ex-army man. I'll send a note to him."

Spur watched White out the window. He walked across the street and stared back at the bank. Then walked slowly toward City Hall.

As Spur observed him, he became aware of someone following White. He recognized the person as Mrs. Trembolt. She carried a large reticule and walked quickly after White. But he moved faster and faster and soon outdistanced Milicent Trembolt even though he didn't know he was in a race.

Spur frowned watching her. She evidently had recovered quickly from the rape or attempted rape he had never found out for sure. He did know there had been no charges filed against her for the death of the Negro.

"Spur, what do you think Don White will do next?" Beth asked.

"What would you do in his place?"

She thought a minute. "I'd come back and rob the bank just before I left town with the rest of the city money."

"Right. Me too. And that's probably what White is planning right now. He should hit you at least by tomorrow afternoon just before your closing time. When is that?"

"Three o'clock."

"I'll try to be around, too." He smiled at Beth. "How old are you, Miss Bank President?"

"Almost twenty. The judge said I could take over

control because I was the only survivor. He gave me some kind of a legal paper I have in the safe.''

"Good. I'm glad it's all legal. From what everyone says, you're doing just fine.''

She smiled and came closer to him and spoke softly. ''Was I fine last night? That's important to me.''

"You were better than fine, you were great. Now get that guard and think about where you could hide some of the cash you have. Not in the vault, somewhere else. Maybe a desk drawer.''

"Good idea.''

"I've got another call to make. Watch for White, but don't try to shoot it out with him. You'll just get your people killed. Except the guard, I mean.'' He grinned and walked out the front door.

Five minutes later he sat in a small room in the side of the school at the Catholic Church and talked with the Mother Superior.

"How long have you been in charge here, Mother Superior?''

"About six years.''

"That goes back to the hard times during the war. You were here then when Father Desmond was assigned to this parish?''

"That's right.''

"I'm investigating a problem here in town during the end of the war. I hope you can help me.''

"I'll do whatever I can, Mr. McCoy.''

"You must remember a defense force raised here called the Mounted Home Guard. Marshal Ludlow organized it and it had as many as twelve to fourteen men in it.''

"Yes, I remember them drilling, riding. I think once we even heard them doing target practice outside of town.''

"Good. Now this next question may be difficult, but I want a truthful answer. Do you remember Father Desmond being a part of this paramilitary group?"

"That would be impossible. A priest could never . . . ."

Spur held up his hand stopping her. "Mother Superior, I don't need a lecture on priestly duties and vows. Was Father Desmond in the Mounted Home Guard? Yes or no."

"No, it would violate his vows."

"Mother Superior, you and I know that Father Desmond had a habit of violating his vows. He was a whiskey priest, a drunk. He also violated his vow of chastity."

"That is not true. I know for a . . ."

Again Spur silenced her.

"Have you made funeral arrangements for Father Desmond?"

"Yes, tomorrow."

"What about arrangements for the girl, Calida?"

Mother Superior looked up sharply, she gasped, then her eyes closed slightly. "So it was you. Sister Evangeline saw someone going toward Father Desmond's quarters early this morning."

She sighed. "This is not an easy task, Mr. McCoy. I do what I think is best for the Church and for my order. What good would it have done to let the marshal see them both that way? It could only have caused hurt and evil."

"I've heard of cases like this before, Mother Superior. I thought you might take care of it, which is why I left so quickly. Father Desmond left a note. Would you like to read it?"

She shook her head. "No. Then I would have more to confess, more to try to forget. But to answer your other question, Calida was returned to her people well to the south. They were told she was attacked by a pack of dogs. They will ask no questions.''

"My first question about Father Desmond, Sister?''

"Yes. Father Desmond slipped off from time to time to ride with the men. He enjoyed it. I liked to see him happy at least once in a while. He had so much sadness in his life.''

"Do you know if the Guard ever attacked another group of men during the closing days of the war?''

"Attacked?''

"Yes. A final jab at the Yankees. One last protesting raid to vent their frustration at losing the war?''

"Oh, I understand. Lots of the town talk I never hear. But this particular one . . . yes, I do remember. Marshal Ludlow was quite open about it. He wanted to strike one last blow at the enemy.''

"And did it happen, Mother Superior?''

"I don't know. Father was gone for a time one night. I remember him coming back very late, it was almost dawn. I was up for my five A.M. prayers. He was tired and *dirty*. He looked worn out. I've never seen him that way before.''

"Did he give any explanations, say anything?''

"Curious, he did. I thought nothing of it at the time. It's a phrase we use with each other when we're feeling low or are having problems. He said, 'Pray for me, Sister.' ''

"That was all?''

"That was enough.''

"Thank you Mother Superior. I assure you that none of this will go any farther. We shall let Father Desmond rest in whatever kind of peace he was hoping to find.''

"Bless you, Mr. McCoy.''

"I'm not here to destroy, or for retribution. But in this case there has been a great wrong done and I am determined to set it right."

"Right can be both powerful and at the same time destroy."

Spur nodded. "Pray for me, Sister," he said then walked out of the room and into the afternoon Texas sunshine.

Marshal Ludlow fell into step beside Spur as he walked down the street.

"You wondering about the priest, too?"

"What do you mean?"

"Why else you jawing with the Mother Superior in there?"

"Maybe I'm Catholic."

"Maybe pigs can fly. What I figure is the old boy slit his own throat and she covered it up, make out like a burglary. Just to keep his reputation."

"I hear he was a whiskey priest," Spur said. "Why would she worry about his rep?"

"She's a woman, I guess. Maybe she had the wants for his privates. I hear whiskey priests get a woman now and then."

"Probably happens. You have any evidence on this priest that points that way?"

"Nope. Not yet. Probably could find some, if I wanted to dig a bit."

"Why not let it be? So if he did kill himself. What good would it do to bring it out with a big story in the paper?"

"Yeah, what the hell."

"You get anywhere on Harry Johnson's killing?"

"Nope. Dead end. Man had no enemies."

"Keep looking, his daughter is unhappy not knowing what happened."

"I can understand that."

"You working on those names for me on the Mounted Home Guard members?"

"Yep. Thought of one more—Bill Jorerdan down at the livery. He trained with us for about two months."

"Keep thinking, I'll be in touch."

Garth Ludlow said he would and watched the Secret Service Agent walk off toward the hotel. He snorted softly. Be a cold day in hell, Spur McCoy when I give you the important names. He paused for a moment, then turned down the alley. He had five minutes to get to the newspaper office for a special meeting.

16

Marshal Garth Ludlow knocked twice on the alley door of the *Record* newspaper office and waited. A moment later someone looked out a small bored hole in the door and then the door opened.

"Garth," Hans said softly. "Damn glad you could come. I think we got trouble."

"I know we damn well got big trouble," Garth said. "That fucking Government agent has been prodding at me, digging into the Guard. We got to do something."

"The others are over here," Hans said. Leading Garth through the unlighted and un-windowed rear shop of the news plant. They wound past a press, and stacks of boxed paper in the two-page newsprint size, and into a small room built in the larger space at one side.

There were four chairs around a table. Two decks of cards and a bottle of whiskey sat in the center of the table.

Zed Hiatt waved at Garth and wiped sweat off his forehead. Beside him Dr. Greenly had just poured himself a shot of whiskey.

"I thought we settled this a few weeks back," Greenly said. "Why is everyone so itchy?" The medical man downed the shot of whiskey and coughed once, then shook his head. "Hans, you've got to get better booze in this place."

"Just because this government busybody is snooping around is no reason to lose our heads. He asked me some questions about Harry. I told him telling the truth right then would have opened up a civil war in town all over again, white versus the blacks. Thought I convinced him."

Ludlow stood at the head of the table as the others looked up at him from where they sat.

"You probably did. Then he talked to some other people in town, lots of people. He's a bastard once he gets a scent. But I don't think it's as bad as it seems. Still we do have a decison to make. Harry got us into this mess by writing that damn letter. I wish I could see it to know exactly how much he told. Not knowing that, we have to strike out a little blind.

"I should have known that Desmond couldn't take the gaff. Any whiskey priest with a twelve year old for his private fucking has got to be unstable."

"We don't know for sure he was dicking her," Hans said.

"Hell, he as much as told me he was," Zed said. "One night he was skunk drunk and he was bragging how many women he'd had. He liked them young thirteen to fifteen, he said. Know for a fact he brought her in from south somewhere. Wasn't even a local Mex."

"So he's gone and no big loss," Dr. Greenly said. "One less share. We're down to four. We've got no worry about Beth. She's set up for life with the bank."

"Are you men thinking it's about time to cash

in?'' Ludlow asked.

"Past time, far as I'm concerned," Dr. Greenly said, "Especially with the bloodhound watching our every move."

"Hell, yes, let's do it," Hans added.

"I'm ready to retire right now," Zed Hiatt said.

"Fine with me, gents." Ludlow looked at them closely. "The problem now is when? Any suggestions?"

"Tonight," Hans said.

The others agreed.

Ludlow nodded. "Sounds soon enough. Remember to bring a shovel, a rifle and a six-gun. We don't want anyone sneaking up on us. We'll have out two guards at all times, and two men working. Damn, we're going to need a wagon."

Ludlow looked around the men. "Who can drive out a wagon?"

Hans waved a hand. "Hell, I rent one now and then to move stuff. I'll get one this afternoon and have it ready."

"Anyone thought what we do after the wagon is loaded?" Ludlow asked. "We don't just split it four ways and drive back into town and unload."

"Christ, more problems," Dr. Greenly said.

"Not problems, just points to be settled before they get to be problems. Planning always pays off." Ludlow stared at the doctor for a moment.

Ludlow shrugged. "I've got that little spread about three miles out of town I own. We'll take it there and then each one of you can move your share wherever you want to."

"What about using it?" Hans asked.

"Just don't try to do anything nearby," Ludlow suggested. "Dallas is as close as I'm going to work any of it."

"Sounds reasonable," Zed said.

They looked at each other. "Meet just north of town at midnight," Ludlow said. "We'll take it from there." Excitement had crept into his voice. "Damn, this is finally going to be over. About goddamned time!"

Zed poured the four shot glasses full of whiskey and they all stood and lifted their glasses.

"To the four of us, to wealth and happiness," they all said in unison. Then they downed the whiskey and looked at each other.

"Damn, I think it's going to happen!" Zed Hiatt said.

Slowly the three men drifted out the back door and went about the rest of their normal day's activities.

At five minutes before three o'clock, Don White and two Negro men slipped into the Johnson Bank. Beth tried to signal to Jim the guard she had hired. He simply nodded to White who he knew was the mayor and turned back to the chair he had been sitting in.

Don White drew a revolver and shot Jim in the back, killing him instantly.

"Nobody move!" White roared. There were three customers in the bank. "You three out here, lay down on your backs on the floor, right now. You have any weapons?"

The two women and one man shook their heads.

"You do and you're dead." One of the black men locked the outside door. The other kept a six-gun trained on the customers. White and the other Negro man jumped the counter. The black cleaned out the teller cages of ready money.

"You tellers, lay down on the floor, now! Beth,

you lay down on that desk. Don't move, any of you or you're dead!''

The teller had finished taking all the paper money from the cages. He stuffed it in a pillowcase he carried and kept his six-gun on the bankers.

White vanished inside the safe and laughed. He found more money than he figured. Quickly he stripped it out of the wooden drawers and dumped the bound packets of tens, fives and twenties into a pillow case he carried.

He passed up the gold. It would be too heavy to carry. He found two more drawers filled with old bills and he swept them into his bag as well. Then he found only empty drawers. He swore, and lifted the sack and laughed, then left the bank vault.

"Nobody move. Don't lift an eyelash." He went up to Beth where she lay on her back on the desk top. For a minute he laughed, then he reached down and fondled her breasts.

"Not a word, woman!" he spat. His hand went lower to her crotch. He spread her legs, then leaned down and lay on her as he kissed her lips. She struggled.

He lifted up, laughed and motioned the Negroes toward the back door. They went down a hall ahead of him. Beth sat up.

"Down!" he thundered lifting his six-gun and turning toward her. She lay down quickly. "Nobody move for five minutes. I got two men with rifles aimed at the front door. Anybody go out there for ten minutes and he's one dead man."

White ran down the hall to the rear of the bank. It was on the corner of the block and the back door was near the street. One of his black men had the door opened. White ran up and pushed him forward.

"Outside, stupid. Let's get away from here!"

The first Negro ran out the door into the alley followed closely by the second. Both had their guns up and ready. White let them get twenty feet ahead. He sent one .44 slug up the hallway into the front of the bank, then reached the door and stepped inside.

A woman jumped around the corner and aimed a double barreled shotgun. She blasted the first round at the Negro who was less than fifteen feet from him.

The double ought buck caught him in the chest and drove him back three feet, blasting six of his ribs into his heart, other slugs chopping his heart and lungs into a mass of spurting blood, shattered bone fragments and splattering tissue.

Without pausing the woman shifted her aim to the second Negro who had lifted his pistol when the second blast of the shotgun caught him. It tore the iron from his hand, shattered his hand and arm and continued forward and almost tore his head off his shoulders. He slammed to the ground six feet from the bank door.

The door had already closed behind Don White. There was nowhere to go but forward. The woman did not take time to reload. She threw the shotgun aside and pulled a foot long butcher knife and charged White.

He had time only to lift his .44 and shoot once. The bullet hit her in the chest, staggered her but she powered forward, the long knife slashing.

White had no time for a second shot before she was on him. The first swipe of the knife severed the arteries and muscles on his right wrist. Fingers relaxed and the White six-gun fell into the dust.

Before White could focus his eyes on the blood spurting wrist, the deadly knife swung again, its razor sharp blade slicing through Don White's neck on the left side. The gush of blood from the carotid artery drenched his shirt and pants as he crumpled to the ground.

The woman fell to her knees, stabbing White, slashing his neck and face, then stabbing again and again in the bloody shirt where his heart should be.

She shuddered and then gasped.

Two men ran into the alley. One of them rushed out to bring the marshal. The other man walked forward looking at the four bleeding and dead bodies.

The woman lifted the knife again, her strength fading quickly now. She swung the knife again, and sliced Don White's nose off his face.

Then she wailed in agony, slumped forward and fell on Don White's silent chest.

Spur McCoy heard the shots. He had been in a store across the street and did not see White or his men slip into the bank. He charged around the corner and into the alley. In one quick glance he knew the two blacks were dead.

Slowly he advanced on the second pair of bodies. He saw the woman and surprise washed over his face. He had seen that dress before today.

He knelt beside the bloody pair and lifted the woman's head. Milicent Trembolt. She had been following White for a reason. She may have followed him all day, figured out what he was going to do, saw him go into the bank and figured White would come out the back way.

Both she and White were dead.

He stood and waved at the crowd. "All right, move back. We can't help these four in any way. Move it back. Did someone go for the marshal?"

One man said the marshal was coming.

Spur pointed at him. "You and you, keep these

people back until the marshal gets here. I need to get into the bank." He checked the two blood splattered pillow cases. When he saw money in them both, he picked them up and carried them into the bank.

He called from the back door.

"Beth. Beth, it's all over. Are you all right in there?"

"Yes! Yes! Most of us are fine."

She flew down the hallway and hugged him. She wouldn't let go. They walked back to the front of the bank.

"Most of us are fine. Jim, the guard, is dead. White shot him in the back without any warning!"

"Sounds like White. He won't hurt anyone ever again."

"You shot him, Spur?"

"No, Milicent Trembolt did. She either shot him or killed him with a butcher knife."

"Oh, dear God!"

"I'm afraid Mrs. Trembolt is dead, too."

"I liked her." Beth wiped sudden tears away. "Will someone come and get Jim?"

"I'll arrange it. I want to get out to that house White had at the edge of town. He must have been ready to run away." Spur kissed her cheek and ran out the back door. The marshal and undertaker were there. He found three horses at the back of the bank. Nobody claimed them. He figured they were White's. He mounted one and rode quickly to the house someone told him the mayor had used.

Just as he came up he saw a small black girl riding away fast on the bay. He let her go.

There was no one else in the house. Spur found the satchel with the city's money in it. There was a blanket roll and a small carpetbag all packed.

Spur picked up the money, searched the house but found no other valuables, and rode back to the bank. He set the satchel on Beth's desk.

"City money, I'd imagine. You'll have to send one of your bookkeepers over to City Hall and check the tax payment records. I'd guess most of this is from the current taxes paid."

"I'd think so."

The bank was quiet. The workers had gone home. The undertaker had carried Jim the guard out and washed the blood off the bank floor. The bodies in back were gone, too. There would be lots of funerals in town the next few days.

"Is it over, Spur?"

"The Carpetbaggers part is over. I'm sure most of the city's money is there. The girl might have taken some of it. Without their dole, the Negroes will drift on to other towns."

"I hope so." She paused. "Now, what about Daddy? Will we ever know?"

"I hope we do. Now I have only one group to watch. The death of Father Desmond may stir these men into action. I'll be watching them."

"What about dinner at my house?"

"Not tonight, Beth. I'm going to be watching every move that Hans Runner and Doc Greenly make."

"I could help. Hard to be in two places at once."

She was right. "You're hired. You watch Doc Greenly. You have a horse and riding clothes?"

"I could ride before I could crawl."

Spur grinned. "Okay, you win. You take Dr. Greenly. Don't let him see you, but don't let him get out the back door or the front without you following him. Can the doctor ride a horse?"

"He can. Told me once he likes to ride. Strange, these men like to ride who don't have to."

"Tonight they may have to."

She reached up and kissed his lips. "I'm going home and dig out my riding clothes. Oh, if the doctor goes somewhere, how do I find you to tell you?"

"If I'm right he'll go the same place that Hans goes. Then we'll find each other." She waved and they went their separate ways from in front of the bank.

17

After the other three men left the back of the news-paper office that afternoon, Hans Runner sat in his big office chair and stared at the wall. It had been a wild, crazy, unpredictable time, the big war. Things had changed, an upheaval had taken place, and for the most part their small town had been passed by this far up in Texas, even by the border raiders.

Then the third raid came by the force of twenty Yankees. They had swept into town, killed three men and scared the rest of the able bodied who could pull a trigger. They had three or four women, used them all night, then raided the general store and the butcher shop and tore off with a wagon full of food and a string of ten stolen horses.

That was the spark that set them off. The very next day a dozen of the men in town got together and demanded that they form some kind of defensive force. Garth Ludlow had been the only man to fight back the night before. He had wounded two of the Yankees before they routed him from the hayloft and chased him ten miles down river. He escaped from the Yankees and rode back into town something of a local hero.

Now they voted him the head of the new Johnson Creek defensive force. He had been at The Wilderness, a classic battle of victory that looked like defeat. He knew what he was doing. A week later he had formed the Mounted Home Guard. Every volunteer had a rifle, a pistol and a good horse. They had trained every day for a week, then once a week after that.

Half the men in town who could ride a horse wanted to be in the Home Guard. At last Garth had tested each man with a rifle. Those who could shoot straight enough qualified for the Home Guard.

They had twenty-five at the time. They were ready. A series of shots, three, then three more was the signal to assemble prepared to fight.

The signal never came.

Hans went to the room at the side of the press and poured himself a shot of whiskey, threw it down and leaned back in his chair.

The Yankee far-ranger patrols evidently pulled back, or moved on. The Mounted Home Guard at Johnson Creek didn't see a Yankee for more than three months. The war was grinding down. More reports of deaths of men in the county. Then two more wounded men came home.

Things were going bad for the Confederacy. When Captain Jones came back home to Johnson Creek wounded in the chest and with just one leg, he said the South had lost the war. It was only a matter of a few months now.

A month later, the news that a detachment of twelve Yankee soldiers had been spotted just north of town caused quite a stir. There was talk of raising the Mounted Home Guard and challenging them, running them out of the county.

Garth had done a lot of fancy talking in the saloons and on the boardwalk. He was all for charging into the damn Yankees. Then that night he got together some of the best men he had behind the livery and did some plain talking.

"Men, I'm sick to death of this damn war, and looks like it's about over. We got us twelve Yankees not five miles from here. I say we pay them a social call. We been training for three months with nothing to shoot at. Who is with me on a little hunting practice?"

Six men stayed. Three went home and Garth made them swear to forget all about it. Garth let the three return home and then turned and stared hard at the five men who stayed with him and were ready to fight.

"This won't be a classic battle, men, and it might wind up being nothing. But by God, we're going to poke them damn Yankees in the ass and let them see how it feels!"

Garth inspected every man. Pistol and rifle and sixty rounds for each. He nodded.

"Let's move out!"

They rode single file, with Garth in the lead. He found the squad of Cavalrymen just where they had been reported, near the well at the old burned out Johnson place.

Garth ordered his men to dismount a quarter of a mile away in a little bunch of cottonwoods. They moved up cautiously and watched the small camp for half an hour.

Garth grinned. One man on guard, and he even had a fire! He must be pretty cocky. Expecting no trouble. He wouldn't even feel the trouble he was getting. Garth waved at the men and they all moved up beside him silently.

"One guard. I'll take him out, them move forward on my hand signal. I'll be in the edge of the firelight. Come in fast but quiet. Got it?"

Garth looked at Father Desmond. He had been surprised when the priest chose to come. "Father, does this bother you? Does it go against your vows?"

"You said I could be your chaplain. If any of you get wounded, I can help."

"Father, if things get tight, I'll need that rifle of yours. You can use it as good as any of the other men here. If it comes down to kill or get killed yourself, you got to decide which one you gonna do."

Hans Runner, Harry Johnson, Dr. Greenly and Zed Hiatt agreed with Garth in a quiet endorsement.

"We'll just see what happens," the priest said.

Garth left them, slipping up on quiet feet toward the well house, then around it to where the guard stood, half in the light, half out. Garth saw the wagon, a big heavy one, with a canvas top and extra wide metal wheels. He wondered what the cargo was.

The squad seemed to be moving it somewhere. Were they its escort and guard, or was it simply supplies for their trip? He would know soon.

He went into a crouch behind the well itself as the guard turned. The Yankee Bluebelly sighed, slung his rifle over his shoulder on the strap and walked to the far side of the camp, then back.

He came within six feet of where Garth crouched. The trained infantryman had out a five-inch skinning-sharp knife and when the Yankee turned his back, Garth sprang forward, took three steps and his left arm whipped around the Yankee throat, half strangling him, cutting off any sound.

Garth's right hand drove the heavy blade down into the Bluebelly's chest, felt the knife slant off a bone and then drive in deep. Twice more he stabbed the soldier, then the man sagged like a limp sack against Garth. He let the body down to the ground quietly and checked. The damn Yankee was dead!

Garth looked over the camp. There were eleven blankets with blue uniforms huddled in them even though it was a warm night.

He signalled the men and they came up quietly. Two went directly to the wagon, cut away bindings inside and some of the canvas which covered everything inside.

Dr. Greenly came back to Garth with a story that made his eyes widen and his pulse race.

"Dr. Greenly, are you sure?" Garth said, his voice breaking with emotion.

"Dead sure. I don't know how much, but more than enough for all six of us."

Garth pulled his men back. Quietly he told them what was on the wagon. They stared at him in amazement.

"Spoils of war, I'd say," Harry Johnson advised.

"Looks like them that takes, keeps," Zed Hiatt said. The other men quietly said about the same thing.

"So we do it," Garth said. He assigned three men to hit each side of the camp where the men were spread.

He cautioned them. "Nobody gets away. We gonna take the wagon and we got to make sure none of these Yankees lives to tell about it. We take them before they can get off a shot. Tough way to go, but as you men know, there's a damn bloody civil war on and in a war men tend to get themselves hurt."

They were told not to fire until Garth did. He gave them plenty of time to get in position. When he saw the faint wave of Harry Johnson, he killed the closest Yankee with a shot to the heart.

The little ranch yard rang with the sound of Sharps and Spencers and a few pistol shots.

"Oh my God!" one Yankee voice screamed. A pistol shot sounded quickly and then all was quiet.

Garth walked up to the fire and built it higher. The other men slowly moved up to the fire. For a time nobody said a word. Their faces showed their sudden baptism by fire in a real war. They were now blooded veterans.

Harry Johnson's face was still white. He said nothing and stared into space for a while then turned his face away from the fire.

Garth had killed enough men that two or three more by his hand made no difference.

Father Desmond looked at Garth and shook his head sadly. Garth did not know if the priest had fired his weapons or not, and he certainly wasn't going to ask him.

Hans Runner grinned at Garth and winked. Hans would be all right. Zed Hiatt looked into the fire. Tears ran down his cheeks and he didn't try to stop them. "My God! Do you men realize we just slaughtered twelve human beings! How can we ever justify this? How can we live with such a crime!"

"It's no crime, Zed," Garth said sharply. "You are a soldier, and this is war. Those men are the enemy. Remember that."

Dr. Greenly came up a moment later.

"All of them are dead, medically, absolutely. What the hell do we do next?"

"Bury them," Garth said. "Deep where they

won't be found for a hundred years.''

They at last settled for a common grave six feet deep in a nearby cornfield. Someone suggested the well, but when the ranch was built back, the well would be cleaned and the bodies would be found.

The digging was easy. They found two spades in the half burned barn. Garth would permit no riffling of pockets of the Yankees.

"They were soldiers, who died in battle. Give them the decency of a plain burial."

While two men dug the grave, the other four worked on the wagon. They hitched up the horses and drove the wagon over to the half burned barn. It took an hour to pull up the floorboards on the front unburned section of the barn. Then they dug a shallow hole under the floor and moved the cargo from the wagon to the hole.

They were done about the time the grave was filled.

With aching backs and sore arms, they put the barn floor boards back in place, then scattered hay and dirt over it.

"The wagon," Garth said. "It's Yankee army from end to end. We have to get rid of it somehow."

"Burn it," Hans suggested.

"Too damn slow," Garth said. "That's heavy wood. It would burn for a day and a half."

After ten minutes of wrangling, they drove the big wagon to a bluff a half mile away, unhitched the horses and pushed the heavy rig off the eighty foot drop. It smashed into pieces on the rocks below.

The four draft horses were unharnessed and turned loose. They would find a home at a ranch nearby quickly enough.

With bone weary bodies, the six men rode back to Johnson Creek, arriving just before sunrise. All six slept the clock around, but nobody seemed to notice it.

The day after that a rider came into town and shouted the news. The war was over! The South had lost. The surrender had taken place almost three weeks before.

That night the six members of the Mounted Home Guard who had killed the Yankees gathered in a side room in back of the newspaper office.

"We shot down those men in their sleep three weeks after the war was over!" Harry Johnson shouted. "We're no better than murderers! We killed them for what they carried."

"We didn't know the war was over!" Garth shouted back. "Nobody knew it. The war was still on for us. It was a wartime fight, pure and simple."

For three hours they argued, came close to blows, and at last Dr. Greenly had the final word.

"Right or wrong, it's done. None of us wants to hang for doing what we thought was a patriotic act. I say we just let it sit. We do absolutely nothing. We act as if nothing had happened and in five, maybe ten years, we get together and settle the matter of the goods on that wagon."

An hour after that they had it worked out. They would watch and wait, but they would also have a poker game on the first Saturday night of every month. It had served as a way of keeping in touch with each other, and to support one if he was starting to break.

They had missed on Harry Johnson. Hans knew they should have seen it coming. None of them had. Father Desmond had been the weak link all along. Hans had been with him. The priest had not fired at the Yankees. Hans had not expected him to. The priest had a lot of other problems besides the Home

Guard attack on that Yankee detail.

Harry Johnson's letter had been another matter. Garth said they had to kill him before he talked. Reluctantly they all agreed. Harry had refused to come to the last poker game. They went to see him instead. All had fired into Harry's body. Hans could not remember who fired the first shot.

By all firing, each one could be labeled the killer, and all would be bound by the pledge not to inform on the others, since he then would be informing on himself.

This time Father Desmond had fired. They had held his hand on the gun and forced him to pull the trigger.

Hans Runner put his feet down and poured another shot from the whiskey bottle on the table. Now almost four years after that murderous night, they would finish it. After tonight it would all be over. The alliance of six men so different yet bound together by a deadly secret, would be ended. They could go their separate ways. Now the four survivors would divide the cargo, and their lives would be changed forever.

Hans stared at the newspaper office again, had one more shot of whiskey and went back to setting type for the next edition of the newspaper.

He heard the story about the bank robbery soon after it happened, and hurried over. He'd have a new lead story for the front page. The big story would happen tonight, and he wasn't going to use it. For just a moment his journalistic ethics reared up and bothered him. He thought of that glorious cargo they had buried four years ago, and told his conscious to take his ethics and get lost in whirlwind somewhere.

18

Marshal Garth Ludlow had arrived at the scene of the five killings shortly before Spur had ridden away. He took care of it systematically. Got statements from Beth, called the undertaker, made a sketch of the position of the bodies and what evidently had happened. Then he told the undertaker to remove the bodies.

Five of them inside of about ten minutes. That was a record for Johnson Creek . . . especially with one of the dead being a woman.

At least there was no killer he had to charge out of town to chase down with a posse. He settled in his chair in the jail and let his hat come down over his eyes. The Carpetbagger problem was over. It had been coming to a head for weeks. If any of the transient blacks were still around next week, he'd run them out of town. Most of them were no accounts anyway.

Then there was tonight.

For a moment he hardly believed that it was finally going to end. The adventure that started almost four years ago was almost over. And he

would never have to work another day for as long as
he lived!

Garth smiled. He could even find a woman, not
just a woman, a beauty! One with a pretty face, and
a sleek little figure and big tits! All his life he had
lusted after women with big knockers. He always
picked the whore with the biggest tits no matter
what the rest of her was like.

Yeah, and he'd get a beauty who liked to crawl
into bed and make love in the wildest ways. He
could teach her that. He would be a good teacher.
Houston maybe, or on to New Orleans.

It would take some time, but hell, he was a young
man, he had plenty of time. After tonight time
would be one more thing that he had plenty of.
Money and time, what a great combination and
what he was going to do!

He had worked hard all his life just trying to find
enough to eat and keep a roof over his head. The war
had helped him that way. Before he went to war he
had been a kid. He was only eighteen when he killed
his first man with a blue uniform. That helped a boy
turn into a man fast.

His old daddy had died when Garth was ten. He
remembered it. The long black carriage and the
singing and wailing. They made him look at the box
in the ground and told him his daddy was in there.
He didn't believe it. His daddy never liked small
places. Nobody could make him climb into that little
box. Anyway he figured his ma was lying to him,
she had lied to him before.

She ran off the next year. He was eleven and
stayed with some shirttail cousins for a spell. Only
the uncle had ten kids of his own and there never
was enough to eat. When he was twelve he ran off
and worked on a ranch for a while. Then he took off

from there again and wound up in Johnson Creek.

He was a swamper for a couple of saloons. By the time he was fourteen he was big enough to do cattle work, and he signed on at the Lazy L, only they lost all their cattle in the drought and he moved on to a new outfit, then came back to Johnson Creek about when the war started.

He returned a hero to Johnson Creek after the war when he fought the Yankee raiders and got himself named town marshal. Hell, he'd done as good a job as the next town marshal. Had a girl for a while, but she married somebody else, a guy with a small ranch. He saw her now and then. She had four kids and another one on the way. Not at all pretty any more.

Big tits! The pretty woman he married had to have big ones he could play with and swing around. Damn! but he liked big tits. Like June had. Yeah. He should see June tonight before they went out to the old ranch.

He changed his mind in an instant.

No! Instead of humping June, what he had to do was kill Spur McCoy!

The damned Government Agent was getting too close. He had figured out most of it. If he kept going he was bound to make one of the last four men crack and tell the whole thing. Zed Hiatt most likely.

Today, or just after dark. He had to put the Sharps slug through Spur McCoy's heart. By the time the government heard about it and sent somebody to investigate, ex-Town Marshal Garth Ludlow would be in Houston!

How to do it? A rifle would be safest. Ludlow prided himself on keeping his long gun eye sharp. He could drive a ten penny nail at fifty yards.

Ludlow dropped his feet off his desk and headed

179

for the door. Automatically he adjusted the hog leg at his side, and made sure the iron would not stick in the leather.

Then he moved outside to the boardwalk and started searching for Spur McCoy. He'd find him and track him. He had to know where he would be this afternoon.

The bank. If he went after the rest of the city money in the ex-mayor's house, he would bring it back to the bank.

Garth Ludlow was half a block from the bank when he saw Beth Johnson and McCoy come out the front door of the Johnson Bank. She locked the door, talked a moment to McCoy, then each went in a different direction.

Ludlow kept half a block behind the federal lawman. McCoy never looked behind him. He wandered down the street, stopping in a small restaurant across from the newspaper office. He took a seat near the front window, and Ludlow saw McCoy evidently watching the *Record* front door as he ate.

Ludlow slipped into the alley and ran to the back of the store beside the newspaper. It was a harness shop. He talked to the owner, Sam Wilkinson, and then said he needed to watch out the front window without being seen.

Sam told him to go ahead. From well back from the window, Ludlow could watch McCoy in the restaurant. Spur noticed each time someone went in or out of the newspaper office.

A half hour later, Spur finished his meal quickly, got up and hurried to the door. Then he came out casually and walked down the street toward the center of town.

Ludlow followed Spur who evidently was trailing

Hans Runner. Strange, Ludlow thought. How had McCoy tied Hans into the group? By the cover-up on Harry's death? Maybe.

If McCoy kept trailing Hans until tonight, the whole project could be in serious trouble.

Ludlow did not have his Sharps, or even a Spencer repeating rifle. He might have to rely on his six-gun. Which would mean a closer confrontation.

Or a closer bushwhacking.

Where was Hans going? He had to get a team and wagon from the livery for them to use tonight. Yes! Ludlow turned down the next alley, and ran down it to the street, turned toward the livery. He could be a half block from the livery before either of the men. There was a six foot high board fence along a vacant area they would have to pass.

If he worked it right, he could let Hans pass, then shoot Spur McCoy at nearly point blank range as he passed.

Ludlow was sweating by the time he trotted to the edge of the board fence. He looked around it. Hans had stopped to talk with someone near the general store. Spur would be killing time behind him.

Ludlow picked out the ideal spot. Half a board was missing on the fence about a third of the way down. He could let Spur pass and still have plenty of room for a killing shot, two or three if he needed them.

Marshal Ludlow risked a peek out the broken board hole and saw Hans walking quickly toward him. Thirty yards behind him, McCoy had just passed the General Store and came forward.

Ludlow paced nervously. He drew his revolver and checked the loads. Yes, five and the empty chamber under the hammer. He wiped sweat off his forehead. He'd never been this nervous before. It would be simple. He had his escape route all figured. Across the vacant lot to the next street, past the old burned out hotel, back to Main Street where he would discard his brown leather vest and throw away his hat, and walk back to the jail and put on new ones of different colors. Simple.

He heard the footsteps as Hans came striding forward. There was a blur as Hans passed the half-board hole in the fence. Then a dozen seconds later, he caught the sound of Spur's boots on the hard packed earth outside the fence. They came closer.

Ludlow moved up to within a foot of the hole in the fence. Now it was time!

McCoy walked past the hole. Ludlow lifted his weapon. He had not cocked it! He thumbed back the hammer to put it on half cock. The click sounded as loud as a lightning bolt in the suddenly quiet street.

At once Ludlow pulled the trigger. As he did he saw McCoy dive for the dirt and vanish from view through the hole. Ludlow's six-gun fired. He knew he had missed. He wanted to go to the hole and fire again and again.

A hot slug slammed through the half inch fence and splintered wood at Ludlow. Then another .44 size chunk of hot lead and another forming a pattern around the hole in the fence.

Ludlow ducked and ran for the other side of the lot. He was almost there forty yards away when he heard the next shot from behind him. It kicked up dust at his feet and he slashed around the edge of the burned out hotel and down to Main Street. Quickly he slid out of his vest, pulled the personal items from the fob pockets and tossed the vest in a burn barrel.

Two minutes later he was sitting behind his desk, slipping into a fresh vest, this one of doeskin, a light fawn color, the best one he owned. He pushed out the spent round and slid another one into the weapon.

He wiped sweat from his forehead and shivered. How the hell had he forgotten to halfcock his six-gun? He shook his head and sat in his chair. He should tell Hans about McCoy following him. He would go up there later on.

Ludlow shivered again and ran past the back door to the outhouse. He was too late. He walked back into the jail stiff legged and gingerly cleaned himself and changed into a fresh pair of jeans.

Damn! This was not getting off to a good start for the day that was going to make him rich!

Spur McCoy heard the metallic click of a six-gun cocking just as he passed a gap in the board fence, and instinctively he dove to the ground and drew his new model Army Remmington at the same time.

The round fired at him missed, splattered dirt into his face and sang away. He fired three shots around the deadly hole in the fence and jumped to his feet. His right boot hit an inch high rock and his ankle turned over painfully. All he could do was hop back toward the fence. He saw a flash of a figure running across the vacant lot.

When he got to the hole he saw only a man of average height in blue jeans and wearing a brown leather vest, blue shirt and brown hat vanishing around the old hotel.

There was no chance Spur could catch him with his ankle hurting. The only description he had would fit half the men in Johnson Creek.

Walk it out, he told himself. He walked forward and then back, and soon the ankle responded. It had been only a slight turn and not a dangerous sprain.

He could still walk and ride.

But he had lost track of Hans Runner. The newsman had been heading somewhere. Spur walked on down the extension of second street but saw nothing ahead but the Livery.

Time enough to check that later. He went to the livery and rented a horse and saddle, rode the animal around a few blocks to get used to the gelding, then rode back to the Livery and asked about Hans Runner.

"Yep, he was in. Said he had some equipment to move and took out a heavy wagon. Don't know what he had that he'd need anything that heavy, but he said it would do. Two horses and a wagon." The livery man looked up.

"Yeah, I know who you are, McCoy. That's why I'm talking to you so plain. Don't want no trouble with the law. Hans hired a wagon now and then. Nothing unusual. Said he'd be done with it sometime tomorrow."

Spur thanked him and rode away. Back at the Johnson House Hotel he tied the bay to the hitching rack out front and went to find himself a rifle. He bought one at the General Store, a good used Spencer that probably came home from the war. He got twenty rounds, and then twenty more and another box of forty rounds for his .44. He might be having a war all of his own before the night was over.

Spur rode his horse down Main Street until he was half a block from the newspaper office and tied him to a rail. He found a chair next to the Overbay General Store and leaned back in it, watching the newspaper office.

Nothing stirred inside or outside. After an hour he got back on his horse and rode around the block.

Behind the paper's back door he found a heavy wagon parked, and two plow horses still in the traces. Runner was going to do something tonight it seemed, or in the morning.

Spur found another vantage point nearly a block away where he could keep out of sight. He put his horse in the stall of an empty shed, and sat near a small clump of native mesquite. It was big enough to hide him and still let him see through.

He wasn't sure why, but Spur figured the wagon would be going anywhere that Hans Runner went. He hoped that the men who killed Harry Johnson had been scared enough to take some action. There had to be some kind of a secret they were hiding. Somehow it involved Harry Johnson and his death.

Spur squirmed on the ground. He might have a long wait. He wished he'd brought along some coffee, or a canteen. A nice cold beer would go good about now. He shook his head. Later. He'd put it down as one he owed himself. When this was all over he had in mind a nice quiet week of nothing to do but sit in the shade and maybe do some fishing. Not much fishing around Johnson Creek.

For a moment he thought of Beth Johnson. Maybe he would just move into her big house and relax for a while.

Beth would have some entertainment and recreation ideas. McCoy grinned just thinking about the sweet little package of woman.

Then he sat up straight. Hans Runner walked out of the rear door of his printing plant and headed for the team and the big heavy freight wagon.

19

Spur watched the newspaperman lift a cardboard box and put it in the wagon, then go back into the printing plant.

What the hell? Spur wondered. Not a big load for the wagon. What was the printer/newsman up to?

Spur watched for another hour and nothing happened. He was tired and sore from sitting on the ground. He walked around the block and saw that the blind was down on the front door of the news office. That usually meant that the place was closed. He checked his Waterbury. It was just past five o'clock. Hans could be having supper somewhere.

He found the newsman in the third restaurant he checked. Spur did it without the man seeing him. He went across the street to the Demorest eatery and had a quick medium rare steak and all the side dishes. He was surprised when they charged him sixty cents for it. Mrs. Demorest explained it was the biggest steak she had and she figured he'd want it.

Spur checked again, and Hans was still eating. When Hans finished, he carried a sack with him as he went directly back to his newspaper plant.

By the time Spur had run around the block to his hiding spot, he saw Hans putting the paper sack in the wagon, then heading back inside his place of business.

Spur settled down for a long wait. He had no idea if they would move tonight, or a week from tonight. The men were getting nervous, he knew that. He wondered if Beth was having any luck watching the doctor.

Four hours later Spur still lay there, sprawled now on the dirt of the alley, half awake half asleep, but aware of every cricket, every door slam, every horse whinny for a block around.

He checked the Big Dipper. It's pointer stars were almost due west of the North Star. That made it about ten P.M. Maybe tonight wasn't the night.

As he thought it, the back door of the news office opened and a man came out carrying a lantern. He lifted it at the door, evidently locking it from the outside, then walked to the team, checked them and climbed up on the driver's seat.

Spur grinned. Maybe tonight after all!

When the man slapped the reins against the big heavy horses' backs, Spur slid onto his own saddle and watched as the rig moved out slowly down the alley. He waited until it turned the corner, then rode out the alley the other way. The wagon would not be hard to find.

He rode slowly down Main Street and saw the rig turn onto Main a block ahead. He kept that interval as the heavy wagon rolled through the mostly deserted town. Only the saloons and gambling houses were showing lights. Three blocks out Main it turned into residential, and there a few of the homes had yellow lights, but most of the hard working folks of Johnson Creek were fast asleep in bed.

Spur let the wagon get farther ahead and when it angled for the north trail toward Indian Territory, he hung back more. They were a half mile north of town when Spur heard horses behind him coming up fast. There were two of them coming hard. He turned and looked through the blackness of the night, and saw the first wink of a pistol shot before he heard the sound, he leaned low on the neck of the bay and spurred him hard.

The big animal surged forward, and Spur angled him off the trail into a copse of cottonwoods and big boulders. He jumped down from the horse and dove behind a boulder as another volley of pistol fire came from thirty yards away.

Spur took careful aim with his .44 and fired.

The first horse in the charge screamed, fell away to the left in front of the second horse and then went down, the rider spinning head over heels. The other horseman pulled up and turned sharply racing back out of pistol range.

For a moment Spur couldn't see the man on the ground. He jumped up then, dodging and darting one way, then the other as he raced back thirty yards to be away from the enemy fire.

Spur sent two more pistol rounds at them, then reloaded. He could not identify the gunmen. He saw through the darkness that the second man was lifted on the horse, then they rode off double on the nag, heading back to town.

Spur made sure they had left, then he searched in the small stand of cottonwood until he found his bay chomping on some late Spring grass. He caught him, lifted on board, and then moved north again. He would ride quietly through the prairie so the newspaper man could not know he was coming.

He pondered the attack. The only explanation he could think of was that somehow Hans knew he was being followed, or *would be followed*, and set up the two guns to come after him.

Spur moved slowly, nearly silently through the no-moon Texas night. He could not hear nor see the wagon. The agent stayed two hundred yards off the main trail. Ahead he saw a small grove of trees upstream on the tiny Johnson Creek. There was enough water in it to flow year round, but in the Texas summer, it was only a trickle.

Spur moved up silently within a hundred yards of the woods and kept his hand around his mount's muzzle. He listened, and at last heard the jangle of harness. The wagon was in the woods waiting for someone. It would make a good meeting place.

Spur pulled back along the trail for a quarter of a mile and stepped down from the saddle. The Big Dipper sank lower in the western sky, but not to the midnight point yet.

The Secret Agent watched, listened and waited. A half hour later he heard a rider moving up the trail. He could not recognize the horse or the man on its back. Spur ground tied his mount and ran softly behind the rider and to one side.

He moved cautiously as he entered the grove of cottonwoods and black oak. There were dozens of wild pecan trees there and they left pods that crunched under foot. He worked through them and ahead saw a small fire.

A voice barked through the darkness.

"Put out that damn fire! You think this is a church picnic?"

Spur recognized the voice. It belonged to Town Marshal Garth Ludlow.

189

"Jeeze, I like a fire," Hans said.

Spur eased closer as the fire died under a storm of kicked dirt.

"You see anything of McCoy?" Hans asked.

"Met my two men on the way back to town. They told me they put at least three slugs in McCoy and run off his horse. They promised me he was either dead or would be by morning. They wanted the other half of the pay."

"You didn't pay them?"

"Hell no! I told them when I saw the body, they'd get the rest of the money. I don't hand out a hundred dollars without getting my money's worth."

"At least he won't bother us tonight," Hans said, sounding relieved. "I heard a dozen or more shots behind me. I know they had a set-to back there toward town."

"You bring some food?" Ludlow asked.

"Damn right, I get hungry, too, you know. In the wagon. But that's for after the digging."

"Where are the others?" Garth asked.

"Not time yet. They got fifteen minutes. Can I smoke?"

"If you got the makings."

"Hell no more of that. I splurged and bought cigars. Have one."

A moment later Spur saw matches flare and then two red glows as the cigars caught fire. He eased back out of the woods and found his horse where he left him. He tied his kerchief around the bay's muzzle so he wouldn't talk to the other horses as they came by.

The two men came together, ten minutes later. Spur let them get into the woods, then swung up on his horse. He started toward the trail when he sensed more than heard another rider. He waited. The horse came out of the gloom slowly and only at the last moment did he realize who it was.

"Beth! What the hell you doing out here?"

"Oh, God! I'm glad it's you, Spur. I was following Dr. Greenly as ordered. That's him up there with Zed Hiatt. They came out together."

"That's the four of them. Two dead and four to go." He paused. "You did fine, now ride back into town."

"Not a chance. These men killed my father. I want to know why. I've got that right."

He paused. She had. "But what if they catch us? They would kill us just as quickly as they did your father. I don't know why, but something out here is damned important."

"That's why I'm coming with you."

He saw the upthrust of her chin, the tight lips, the determination flashing out of her eyes even in the faint light.

"I guess the only way I can stop you is to run off your horse and hogtie you to a tree."

"You wouldn't do that."

"No, but I should. If you get yourself killed out here I'll just be mad as hell at you."

She laughed softly. "I'll be furious about it myself. Let's get going. Did they meet in the grove?"

"Yes. We'll go around this side, slow and easy." He tied both horse's muzzles with bandannas. "We don't want any horse talk if they smell the other mounts."

She nodded and they walked the horses forward slowly. When they were at the far side of the grove, they heard the jangle of harness as the two plow horses tugged the heavy wagon out of the trees and angled north on the trail again.

"Any ranches out here?" Spur asked.

"A few farther on. Another two miles or so is a ranch my granddad owned. I guess it's mine now. It was burned out thirty or forty years ago and never built back. Indians I guess. But I still pay county taxes on it."

A half hour later they knew the wagon was headed for the old Johnson ranch. When they saw the wagon pull up near the shell of a barn on what Beth said was the old place, Spur and Beth dismounted and ground tied their horses about a quarter of a mile away. Spur took his rifle and all of his shells and then moved up cautiously.

By the time they got there, all four men had lit lanterns in the old barn and were busy lifting the floor boards of the unburned part.

"Beth, did your father ever mention anything happening up here during the war? Any kind of action, or a fight, or maybe some Yankees camped out here?"

"He didn't say anything like that. I do remember somebody said he found a Yankee army wagon wrecked below a cliff around here somewhere." She frowned in the soft night light. "Seems like there was some talk about a patrol of Yankees around here once about at the end of the war, but I can't remember."

They had moved up within fifty yards of the men in the old barn.

"You stay right here," Spur told her. "Did you bring a gun?"

She showed him a small caliber six-gun, maybe a .32 caliber.

"Good, can you use it?"

She nodded. "Daddy wanted me to learn how to

shoot it. I can."

"Good. Stay right here or I'll spank you. I'm going to sneak up closer and find out what's going on. I'll be back."

She caught his sleeve. "Spur McCoy, you be careful. I don't want any bullet holes in that wonderful body of yours."

He grinned and slipped away.

Spur moved to the old well, then forward again until he could see into the open door of the barn. They had half the two-inch floor board planks lifted off and the two men were digging. Spur waited. Soon all four men were in the hole throwing out dirt.

"Damn, I hit something hard!" Hans shouted.

"Me, too!" Zed yelled. "We must be almost there."

A few minutes later as Spur watched, the two men lifted out a long narrow box. It was the kind of crate the army used to ship rifles.

The men heaved the heavy box onto the side of the hole and eagerly opened the heavy hasp. For a moment all four stared into the box. Then Garth picked up something.

Spur saw it gleam in the lamplight. There was no question what it was.

Gold!

Spur had seen a bar like that before. It was a ten pound gold bar in its purest form. Had they found a wagon full of gold?

Spur lifted the rifle. Strategy. They would be well armed.

Doc Greenly took out a bar of gold and hoisted it. He sat down quickly. "Christ! This one little ten pounds of gold is worth over three thousand, three hundred dollars! That's more than I take in in three years!" He shook his head. "Damn, I've got to piss before I wet my pants."

"You're rich enough you can take a leak anywhere you want to!" Zed shouted.

"Rather do my privates in private," Doc said. He put the gold bar back in the box gently and headed into the darkness. He came toward Spur.

Spur tracked the short, red-haired doctor and when he stopped and turned away from the barn, Spur moved toward him silently. Doc was totally relaxed letting the urine flow when he heard something behind him.

Before he could turn, Spur McCoy's left arm wrapped around his throat, jerked him off his feet and dragged him away from the barn. Thirty yards back from the diggers, Spur let up the pressure on Doc Greenly's throat. He rasped for breath.

Spur whispered in his ear. "Not a word, Doc, or I slit your throat ear to ear, you understand?" The man nodded.

Spur tied his big handkerchief around the doctor's mouth gagging him. Then he tied the man's hands behind his back with rawhide and his feet as well.

Beth slid up out of the gloom.

She stared at Doc for a moment then slapped his face so hard his head jolted to one side. Spur grabbed her.

"Not now!" he whispered to her sharply. "He'll have his day in court, then he'll hang. Don't make any more noise. We've got three more of them to capture. Agreed?"

The anger faded from her eyes, and she nodded.

When Spur got back to his vantage point, he saw the three men hoisting box after box out of the hole. How much gold was there?

He lifted his rifle, went into a prone position and sighted in. He had two of the men in the open. Quickly he fired one shot over their heads.

"Freeze right where you are, otherwise you're all dead." Spur bellowed.

Garth dove into the hole out of sight. Zed lifted his hands.

"Don't shoot, oh, God, don't hurt me!"

Hans Runner went for his six-gun at his hip. Spur moved his sights slightly and drilled a .52 caliber slug through Runner's right shoulder. The force of the round knocked him backwards over the boxes of gold. He sat up holding his shoulder.

"Damn you, McCoy! You're supposed to be dead!"

"They missed me, and lied to you. The easy way out."

There was no comment. "Doc is all tied up out here, don't expect him to help you. Give it up, Garth."

"Not a chance, McCoy. We figure we've got a ton of gold here. And it's ours. War loot. Finders keepers. We'll kill you if we have to."

"Big talk for a man pinned down and nowhere near his rifle."

"Been in worse spots," Garth spat.

"Hiatt!" Spur yelled. "Get out of there. Throw down your gun and get out here in the dark."

"No!" Garth screamed. He lifted and fired a shot at Hiatt but the big man was already running into the darkness.

Garth shot out two of the lanterns. Spur ran forward to the very edge of the barn. He could see into part of the hole. He spotted Garth's legs. Spur sighted in. One leg moved. He changed his sighting and fired. The bullet smashed into Garth's right leg, slicing through muscle and tissue but missing the bone, bringing a wail of anger and fury from the town marshal.

195

"Damn you, McCoy!" Garth screamed. He shot out the last lantern and the darkness was complete inside the barn shell.

Spur closed his eyes for a moment, then opened them. He turned his head with his right ear toward the hole. Someone moved. He forgot where Hans Runner was.

"You'll never make it, Garth. Give it up and have a chance to live."

"A jury in this town? No chance in hell I'd make it." He fired twice over the lip of the hole. Spur drew his revolver and put three rounds into where he thought the hole was. One slug hit a wooden box.

"Not even close!" Garth bellowed.

As Garth spoke, Spur sensed that he had moved. There was an open space beyond the hole and the pile of boxes that he guessed must be filled with gold. If Garth tried to run he would go out through that open space. It showed a lighter sky behind the dark sides of the barn and the interior.

Garth would silhouette himself against the sky if he tried to run that way.

"No chance you can make it, Garth. I've got a posse of fifteen men coming out. I figured on midnight."

Garth did not reply. Spur listened. He heard the scrape of a boot on a rock or a timber. Yes a timber. Garth was moving toward the light. Spur concentrated on the lightness of the far opening where the barn side had burned away. He brought up his six-gun to cover the area and held it with both hands, his left locked around his right wrist.

Another scrape.

"You don't have much time left, Garth. Where will you run to?"

The ex-soldier took advantage of the sound of

Spur's voice to make his try. His feet skidded on a rotted timber, then one toe caught and he was up and running for the burned out side of the barn.

It was twenty feet. Spur caught him the moment he lifted from behind the pile of timbers. Ten feet toward the door he was a black blob against the lighter sky. Spur fired twice so fast the shots sounded like one roar.

Spur saw the effect of the first .44 slug. It caught Garth in the shoulder high up on his back and drove him forward. The second round lanced through the middle of Garth's back and he went down with a faint skidding sound that was drowned out by the pistol shots inside the old barn.

Spur stood as still as a stone pillar. He held his breath listening.

A groan drifted back to him. The man had not moved. Slowly, with his weapon up, Spur McCoy edged forward toward Garth Ludlow. In the pale shaft of light from the night sky that slashed into the barn through the opening, he saw Garth spread eagled on the far part of the barn floor that had not been torn up.

"Help me, McCoy!" Garth said.

McCoy saw the growing pool of blood under Garth. He wasn't faking. Spur knelt down beside the wounded man.

"I'll help you, if you tell me about the gold. It was a Northern detail bringing in gold from California?"

"Our best guess," Garth said softly.

"And you hit them before or after you knew about the gold?"

Garth told him.

"You four and Harry Johnson and Father Desmond?"

"True. It was just one last jab at the Bluebellies.

Oh, God that hurts!" He swore for a minute. "Roll me over, Spur. Don't cotton to dying staring at the dirt."

Spur eased him over, saw blood on his chest.

"Passel of stars out there," Spur said.

"Whole shit pot full," Garth agreed. He coughed and spit out blood.

"Damn we had it worked out. We figured a ton of gold. That much gold is worth six hundred, sixty one thousand four hundred and forty dollars!" Garth looked at Spur. "That's one thousand three hundred and seventy-eight years of pay for a cowhand at forty dollars a month wages and found."*

"Was it worth the try?"

"Damn right! I grew up dirt poor, McCoy." He coughed again, a great gout of blood spewed from his mouth.

"Dying, McCoy. I'm dying, you know that?"

"True."

"Worth a try for more than a half million dollars! Damn right. I'd do it again. And the war was still on. It was our patriotic duty to kill them Bluebellies."

He looked up at McCoy.

"Gold . . . McCoy. A ton of gold!" He coughed again, then blood filled his mouth, he let out one last rush of air and his eyes stared at the stars that he would never reach.

Spur ran back to where Beth waited. She had Zed Hiatt lying face down on the ground, his hands behind his back.

*Ton of Gold at $20.67 an ounce (1837 to 1934) equaled $661,440.00. 16 ounces to a pound.

"That's three," Spur said. "What about Hans Runner?"

"Over there, damn near bleeding to death," a soft reply came not ten feet from them. Spur moved cautiously.

"Got no gun, get over here and try to stop this damn blood!"

Spur found him leaning against the pump house. His arm was a mass of blood. Spur felt for the wound. Pressed a piece of Hans's shirt against the gash and bound it with another strip of his shirt.

"You'll live. Where's your gun?"

"Out there somewhere."

Spur searched him, found a small derringer and pocketed it.

"Stand up and move up by the barn. I'll get one of those lanterns working. Lucky he didn't burn down the rest of the barn."

Doc Greenly and Zed Hiatt looked at Spur in surprise when he told them what they were going to do.

"Don't think I'll do that," Zed said.

Spur pushed the muzzle of his .44 hard up under Zed's chin where the fleshy part is tender.

"Zed, you do like I tell you, or I'll blow your head off right here, right now! Is that a good enough reason for you?"

20

Spur untied Doc Greenly and led him and Zed up to the barn. He found a lantern that would work, and put the two men to carrying the boxes of gold to the back of the freight wagon.

"Stack it in there close and tight," Spur told them. "Just like it was yours, which it isn't. It belongs to the United States Government."

The two men grumbled and complained. Beth came up and watched them, her eyes angry as she held the six-gun in her hand. It was enough to keep the workers moving.

Spur picked up a shovel and dug out the last four boxes of gold and hoisted them to the top of the pit.

Spur opened one of the boxes and counted the bars of pure gold in it. There were ten bars. He counted the boxes, twenty of them. If each box had ten bars that would be a ton.

A ton of gold! It was almost enough to make a man forget his loyalties, to forget about the Secret Service and high tail it into the mountains of Colorado and live a life of luxury.

Almost enough.

When they had the twenty boxes spread over the floor of the freight wagon evenly, Spur tied Doc's hands and told him to crawl on board. They lifted Garth's body into the wagon and wrapped it in a canvas. Spur put the wounded Hans Runner in the box, too, and tied their horses on behind.

The sun was just beginning to taint the eastern horizon when they washed up in a bucket of well water and headed back toward town.

At the small cottonwood grove just north of Johnson Creek they parked the wagon, put the prisoners on horses and draped Garth Ludlow over his mount and tied him on.

Beth was amazed. "You leaving a ton of gold sitting in the wagon that way, unprotected?"

"I'll be back in about twenty minutes." Spur said. They rode quickly into town, Spur appointed one of the town men as a deputy to watch the jail and he deposited the three men in one cell. Then he rode back to the wagon of gold.

At the cottonwood grove he cut three fifteen foot tall trees with lots of branches and tied them behind the wagon. Then he drove off toward a draw he had seen on the ride in. He backed the wagon next to a steep wall that looked like it was ready to collapse. Spur unhitched the horses and drove them away from the wagon, then he climbed the wall with one of the shovels and began creating a landslide.

He worked for twenty minutes before he had the first fall started. Then he made another, and within a half hour he had loosened enough dirt and rocks from the side of the bluff to surge down and completely cover up the freight wagon. Spur drove the horses off, used the cottonwood branches to dust out all sign of the tracks, and then mounted up and led the draft horses as he rode back to town.

He turned in the three animals to the livery and said he would take responsibility for the added rent on the freight wagon that Hans took out. The livery man lifted a brow, but said nothing.

Spur went up to his room and washed up, put on clean clothes and then went down to the jail.

Doc Greenly had asked for supplies from his office to fix Hans's arm. It was bandaged and he was in good shape.

Spur sat down with the town's only lawyer, and stared at the three prisoners in their cell.

"I need to know exactly what happened the night Harry Johnson was murdered," Spur said.

Hans laughed. "You asking us to put a noose around our necks? Not a chance."

Doc Greenly shook his head. "You'd have to prove anything that might have happened. Going to be extremely hard."

Zed Hiatt asked to go to the outhouse. The newly appointed deputy unlocked the door, but once outside the cell, Zed went to Spur instead.

"Put me in a different cell, and I'll tell you exactly what happened to Harry. I don't care any more. It's bound to come out anyway. I'll tell you precisely what the five of us did. How we shot Harry Johnson."

Hans screamed at Zed, swore at him in three languages, at last slumped down and shook his head.

Doc Greenly laughed without humor. "It was a gamble, the biggest I ever took in my life. It almost worked. They can't hang me, I didn't fire the first shot. All they can convict me of is conspiracy to cover up a murder. He died instantly when Garth shot him the first time. I touched his throat. I know. All the other four of us did was shoot into a dead man. I don't recall that as being a crime."

Spur had been expecting some such defense. "The conspiracy charge will get you five or ten years, Doc, as well as Zed and Hans. You'll all be old men when you get out. If you get out. I think Harry would have liked the punishment."

"What about the army wagon?" Zed asked.

"I don't know anything about an army wagon. If there's an army wagon around here somewhere, the army will come and claim it." Spur looked at the other two prisoners. "Have either of you seen an army wagon around here lately?"

They both shook their heads. "I didn't think so. If there was a wagon it's hidden so well it would take an army to find it. Certainly there is no chance that three men in jail could tell anyone on the outside where it might be."

Spur tapped the lawyer on the shoulder. "Get those complaints of murder and conspiracy drawn up and over to the county seat this afternoon. Let's move on this quickly. I can't be in town more than another week."

Outside Spur stretched. He needed a good night's sleep. First he had to send an official letter to the army post outside Dallas. He needed an escort of twenty-six troopers. He got paper and pen from the desk clerk and wrote the letter, asking the Post Commander to check Spur's credentials with Gen. Wilton D. Halleck in Washington D.C.

He asked for the mounted escort at the earliest possible time, no later than seven days from receipt of the notice which would arrive by stage. He dated it, signed it, added his title, U.S. Army Colonel, retired, and his Secret Service number and sealed it.

The letter left on the morning stage for Amarillo and points East.

Spur had just finished his noontime meal in the hotel dining room when a young boy handed him a note. It was sealed in a pale pink envelope that smelled of rosewater.

Inside in a delicate hand was a note, also on pale pink paper.

"McCoy. I'm bathed, and rested, I'm hungry but not for food. How fast do you think you can pack your bags and move your things up to my guest room? If the guest room doesn't sound good enough you can have half of the master bedroom.

"Can't wait to have you in my clutches again. Oh, yes, I also want to know the last of the grisly details, and where you hid that wagon." It was signed, President Grant.

Spur folded the envelope and slid it in his pocket. He left a tip for the watiress and went upstairs and packed. He checked out and hired a boy to take his bag to the Johnson house. Then walked up the street.

The army would arrive, dig out the gold and return it to the U.S. mint in Philadelphia which is where it was probably headed for four years ago.

The army would demand an investigation into the death of the patrol, which would be duly recounted as an act of war before the end of the conflict, and it would be laid to rest.

Spur picked a rose from a convenient rose bush on the way to the Johnson place, and held it out as he was let in the door.

Beth smiled at him and led him upstairs to the master bedroom.

"I hope you're going to stay for the trial," Beth said after she kissed him on the cheek. "The judge won't be through town for another month on his circuit."

Spur smiled.

"I'll need at least a week to find out exactly what those men did and how they killed Daddy. And then you have to tell me how you put it all together. That will take a week . . . or . . . so."

Spur McCoy was thinking along the same lines. But he could count on a week, maybe eight days, before a telegram caught up with him by stage and he would be off on another assignment.

But until then . . .

He bent and kissed Beth Johnson's saucy lips. "You are a tease," he said. "A real Texas Tease."

She caught his arm and fell backwards on the big, soft featherbed, pulling him with her.

"Sir, I may be a tease, but at least I know how to deliver."

"You shall," he said, easing down on top of her. "You may be so sore you won't be able to stand up. You said you wanted to try that as I recall."

"Yes, let's try!" she squealed.

They did.